NOTICE PERIOD

FREEDOM WAS A STEP AWAY

MOHAN BACHHETY

Contents

Acknowledgements

This book is dedicated to every reader who found a reflection in these pages—this book is for you.

Thanks to Yogesh Mishra for his sharp proofreading and keen eye for detail.

Special thanks to Sohan Bachhety and Rohan Bachhety for their thoughtful logical corrections and for enriching the narrative with deep insights drawn from their corporate experiences. Without their contributions, this book might never have reached completion. Their clarity of thought and nuanced feedback helped shape the very soul of these pages.

Prologue

Last year, I went to Jaipur for a week—roamed around, explored different places. But no matter where I went, my laptop was always with me. Office meetings, Zoom calls, presentations—all of it. After a whole day of sightseeing, I'd return to my hotel, open my laptop, and dive into emails and discussions.

Before I knew it, the week was over. I had originally planned this trip because I was writing a book about historical places—I wanted to experience them firsthand, to make sure I captured their essence accurately. But what I didn't know was that the real story waiting for me wasn't about forts and palaces. It was something entirely different. A single incident on my way back changed everything.

And that's how this book—**Notice Period**—was born.

It happened in Manesar, while I was heading home. I had lost my way. My phone's battery had died, shutting down Google Maps. With no way to navigate, I looked around for help and spotted a young man standing by the roadside. He was well-dressed, coat, pants, tie—looked sharp, looked dependable. Good build, professional air. Seemed like the right person to ask for directions.

I slowed down, pressed the brake, and rolled down the window.

"Hello Bhai, Does this road lead to Delhi?" I asked.

The man stepped closer. His face was calm, with a soft smile. "Bhai Sahab, You're on the wrong road. Drive ahead, you'll find a crossing. Take a left, then a right, and you'll hit the highway."

I wasn't entirely convinced. If I messed up again, I'd waste more time, and I had a meeting in Delhi I couldn't afford to miss. So I thought of another solution.

"Where are you headed?" I asked.

"I need to go to Delhi too, but I'm waiting for a cab."

"Hop in. You can guide me, and we'll run Google Maps on your phone. My battery's dead, phone's off. Left my charging cable in the hotel this morning, thanks to my usual rush."

He agreed, and settled into the seat.

"What's your name?" I asked.

"Gaurav," he replied, then went silent.

He didn't seem like much of a talker. But I had to keep the conversation going—otherwise, I'd start feeling drowsy behind the wheel. I'd already been driving alone for three straight hours without saying a word to anyone, and the silence was beginning to weigh on me.

To make things easier, I decided to introduce myself first. "I'm Mohan Bachhety. I'm an author. Went to Jaipur for a trip and am heading back now."

"Oh," Gaurav said, nodding slightly. "I've heard your name before—at a book fair. My friend and I went last year. He even bought your book, "The Guilt". I didn't get a chance to read it myself, but he did. He appreciated the work you did in that book."

My trick worked. Just as I had expected—once I started talking about myself, Gaurav naturally opened up.

And with that, our conversation shifted into a comfortable rhythm.

The road ahead still stretched long, but at least now, the silence wasn't unbearable.

Just then, I saw a crowd gathered ahead. I pressed the brake, slowed the car, and pulled over to the side.

The police were trying to move the protestors off the road, making sure traffic kept flowing and the highway didn't get blocked. Every person in the crowd was holding a placard, shouting slogans—

"Fulfill our demands! We want freedom! Take back your policies!"

There were different variations, but all carried the same frustration. Among them, a massive banner stood out—

"MPS Group Limited, Workers' Union, Manesar, Haryana."

I felt a slight tension creeping in. I turned to Gaurav. "Looks like they've blocked the road. I hope I don't get delayed."

But Gaurav wasn't worried. He was smiling—actually, more like **grinning**.

I glanced at him, puzzled. His smile had only widened.

"Inko azadi chahiye(They want freedom)," he said casually.

Then, out of nowhere, **he burst into laughter.**

"What's so funny?" I asked, surprised.

He leaned back, shaking his head. "I just got my freedom."

"What do you mean?"

That's when Gaurav told me everything—why he was standing there waiting for a cab, how he ended up in Manesar, and "what exactly '**freedom**' meant to him".

Listening to his story, I didn't even realize when I had reached Delhi.

By the time I parked, the meeting I was supposed to attend didn't matter anymore. I canceled it instantly. There was only one thing that needed to be done.

I had to write his story.

And that story is the one you are about to read next!!!

CHAPTER ONE

RESIGNATION

Gaurav was sitting quietly. His face looked tired. Dark circles. Faded smile. A body carrying too much burden. Not just sad—lost. His eyes held pain, like a weight pressing down on his chest. Any moment, he could break.

Once, he was strong. Once, he felt alive. Now, his body felt weak. His muscles were gone. Thirty-four years old—but he looked forty-five.

He was staring at a photo on his phone. Ten years ago. Back then, he had energy. Back then, life felt different.

He was thinking.

"Will my life always be like this?

Office. Deadlines. The same insults. The same pressure.

Every four months—a new project. Always urgent. Always stressful.

I can't even go home on time. Is this really life?

Rules, schedules, time limits. Feels like a cage.

Every day, I lose myself a little more.

When did I stop laughing?

When did I become this?

I don't feel like living anymore.

The burden of the office has drained my will to live. Every day, it suffocates me a little more.

And home? That's no better. The endless fights with my wife have left me broken from the inside. There's no escape. No peace.

Sometimes a cowardly thought crosses my mind— I feel like jumping from the office terrace and taking my own life. It is better to die than to live like this."

Just then, his phone rang.

"Hello," Gaurav said the moment he answered the call.

"Left the office yet?" Ruby asked from the other side.

"No, still here. Leaving in a bit."

"Gaurav, it's already 7 PM. The guests will start arriving by eight. You were supposed to leave early today!"

"Please don't stress me out, Ruby. I have work pressure. Need to finish something first, then I'll leave."

"You always have work pressure! Just tell your boss it's Khushi's birthday today. No need to even say you need to leave early—the office timing is 10 to 7. It's already past time. Just leave!"

"Ruby, hang up now." His voice was frustrated as he disconnected the call.

He placed his phone on the desk, leaned back in his chair, and clasped both hands behind his head. His eyes were fixed on the laptop screen, but his mind was somewhere else.

It was Khushi's birthday today. His little girl was turning three. A small party had been planned at home—just four or five close relatives. Her first birthday had been a grand affair, celebrated at a fancy restaurant. But this year, Gaurav didn't have the time. Work had consumed him.

His gaze remained locked on the screen. He needed to leave, but how?

Just then, a voice snapped him out of his thoughts.

"Gaurav, done talking on the phone? Get back to work. No matter what, this project has to be delivered today."

It was Kundan Jha , his project manager. Twenty one years in the company, and Kundan's words carried weight.

Kundan's dusky complexion and army-style haircut gave him a certain harshness, as if he lacked even the slightest trace of empathy. His voice had an ever-present stiffness, devoid of emotion—just enough to ruin anyone's mood within seconds.

Gaurav's mood was already bad, and now, after hearing Kundan's curt comment, he was boiling with frustration. He pushed his chair back and stood up.

"Sir, this work will take at least four to five more hours. Getting it done today is impossible. Let's tell the client we can deliver it tomorrow."

If Gaurav said something couldn't be done today, it meant it really couldn't. No drama, no excuses—just facts.

He wasn't the kind who misjudged timelines. In fact, his estimates had a reputation—never missed, never off. If Kundan gave a deadline of 15 days, Gaurav would quietly finish it in 10. If the client was promised 6 months for delivery, and Gaurav was leading the project, it would get done—within 5 months. No questions asked.

That was the kind of precision he worked with. Sharp. Reliable. So much so, no one dared raise a finger at his work.

But this time, things were different. Kundan, in his overconfidence—or maybe to impress the client—had promised a delivery date without checking with Gaurav first. And now, the project was running behind schedule, and naturally, Kundan was fuming.

Kundan shot him a cold glare. "Are you out of your mind? We can't tell the client anything. Your salary comes from them, so stop making excuses and just finish the damn work."

"Sir, it's my daughter's birthday today. There's a party at home."

The office was almost empty. Most of the staff had already left, except for two seats—one occupied by Kapil Sharma. He had become one of Gaurav's closest friends over the years. Both of them had joined the company on the same day, four years ago. That shared beginning had naturally strengthened their bond.

Kapil was slim, but his smooth hair added to his personality, making him look even more refined. His fair complexion enhanced his features, giving him an almost effortless charm. His lean frame made him appear taller than he actually was, adding to his presence without him even trying.

It had become routine—Kapil and Gaurav wrapping up work together, stepping out of the office at the same time. A cigarette, some useless office gossip, and then they'd go their separate ways—one home, one back to the mess of corporate life waiting for them the next day.

Tonight, Kapil was still sitting there, waiting. He knew Gaurav would be heading out any minute now. He always did.

But today felt different.

Kapil was listening to everything—every word exchanged between Kundan and Gaurav.

He wasn't part of the conversation, but he could feel the tension. The weight in Gaurav's voice, the sharpness in Kundan's tone. It wasn't the first time something like this had happened.

Kapil had seen Gaurav go through this routine over and over—working late, taking pressure, swallowing frustration.

"Listen, Gaurav. If you're not enjoying your work or don't feel like doing it, just say so. I'll move you to another team. Whatever it is, speak openly," Kundan said, locking eyes with him.

"Sir, there's a function at home. That's why I asked to leave early. I know the work is urgent, but it won't get completed today anyway, so what's the point in staying late?" Gaurav replied politely, trying to keep his frustration in check.

Kundan glanced at the clock. "It's just 7:30. If you work properly, it will be done in three hours. That means you'll be free by 10:30. I have a client call at 11 PM. I need this project finished—no matter what."

That was the worst part about working for a US-based company—their office hours never matched India's. When it was 2 PM here, they were just starting their day. And today, the client's meeting was scheduled at 11 PM India time.

Gaurav sighed. "I'll try, sir," he said, his voice carrying the weight of defeat.

"Great. Just fix the issue."

Gaurav gestured for Kapil to leave.

Kapil had already packed his laptop bag, ready to head out. Without wasting a second, he stood up, shook hands with Gaurav, and made his way toward the exit.

Gaurav's frustration was clearly visible. He wasn't the kind of person who would tolerate taunts or bow down under pressure. But for the last few years, that's exactly how life had been for him. He was bulky in build and hot-tempered by nature. Yet, circumstances had forced him into silence. He barely spoke to anyone—just did what was required and kept to himself.

Gaurav had barely opened his laptop for a minute when he shut it again and walked toward the cafeteria. He grabbed a coffee, picked up a cigarette, and headed to the terrace.

He took a sip of his coffee, then a drag from his cigarette. The smoke curled upward, disappearing into the sky. A few minutes passed like this—coffee, smoke, silence—until he started feeling a little better.

Finally, he flicked the cigarette butt onto the floor and crushed it under his shoe, grinding it down with an intensity that made it seem like he was crushing his problems along with it.

Back at his desk, he tried to focus, but his mind kept drifting to the birthday celebration happening back home. He wished he could be there. But work had to be done, and it had to be delivered today. No choice.

He had barely settled in when the voice came again—sharp, impatient.

"How much is left?" Kundan Jha demanded.

"Sir, I'm doing it. Still some work left," Gaurav replied, his voice subdued.

"Hurry up, man."

"Yes, sir."

Gaurav took a deep breath and stretched his fingers before placing them back on the keyboard. The weight of the pending work loomed over him like a storm cloud, pressing down, suffocating. The ticking clock in the corner of his screen felt louder than it should, each second slipping away, mocking him.

The office was quieter now, save for the occasional footsteps echoing through the hallway and the distant hum of a coffee machine. His shoulders stiffened as he pulled up his incomplete task. He had to deliver tonight—no delays, no excuses. His phone buzzed beside him. A message from home. He didn't even look; he knew what it was. Birthday photos, laughter, warmth—all things that seemed so distant from the cold office chair he was glued to.

Gritting his teeth, he opened his project file. The numbers blurred. His mind fought the exhaustion, but the fatigue was relentless. He clenched his fists, shaking off the sluggishness. Focus. This was crunch time.

Kundan's earlier words echoed in his mind—"Hurry up, man."

Gaurav tapped away furiously at his keyboard—running checks, debugging, fixing one error after another. Every time he thought it was done, another issue popped up, like the code was playing whack-a-mole with him. The task was a monster—complicated, stubborn, and totally unforgiving.

9 PM.

His eyes flicked to the clock. That was it. He couldn't take it anymore. The pressure at work had been choking him for weeks. And now, on top of that, his wife had called twice, her tone sharper each time. The party at home was full—ten, maybe twenty people had already come. His daughter's birthday. He had planned it. Send the invites. And yet, he was the only one missing.

Frustrated, he hit submit on whatever half the work he could manage.

He slammed his laptop shut and threw it into the bag like it had just insulted him. Wrapped the charger like a tangled snake and shoved it inside. No careful packing today. No double-checking. He just wanted out.

Kundan shouted,"Is that done?"

"No sir, but I need to go ." Gaurav said rudely , and left.

He walked out of the office, the weight of unfinished work clinging to his shoulders—but heavier still was the guilt of being absent from the one place he actually wanted to be.

Rushing through the exit, he walked briskly toward the parking lot and slid into the driver's seat of his car. His hands moved fast—seatbelt, ignition, gear—like muscle memory in action. But just before turning the key, he paused and checked his phone, a strange calm settling in after the storm.

Just as he had expected—photos from home. The birthday celebration is in full swing. Laughter, cake, decorations. A world completely opposite to the one he had just spent hours in.

But there was something else. A long message, from his wife Ruby-

"I knew it. You were never going to come. You never really cared about us, did you? The whole family was here, and I had to sit there, humiliated, answering the same question over and over—'Where is Gaurav?' What was I supposed to say? Another excuse about your work?

Do you even know what responsibility is? Do you realize how lonely this house feels without you? But you don't care, do you? You only care about yourself. Have you ever stopped to think about what you're doing? Is life just about work? One day, you'll realize what you've lost. And by then, it'll be too late."

Reading his wife's message, Gaurav's mood spiraled again. He had barely escaped the suffocating work pressure, but now this—the guilt, the frustration, the helplessness. His chest tightened. He stopped his car at a stop near his office , roadside tea stall and got off.

"Chotu, one tea and a cigarette," he said to the boy sitting behind the counter. No one really knew the kid's real name. Everyone just called him *Chotu*.

"Tea will take two minutes," *Chotu* said, handing him the cigarette without asking. He knew exactly which one Gaurav smoked.

Gaurav leaned forward, lit his cigarette from the flickering flame tied to the stall with a thin wire. He took a deep drag, exhaling slowly, trying to clear his mind.

"*Bhaiya*, you're late today. Working overtime?" *Chotu* asked, curious.

"Yeah, man. These corporate bloodsuckers just won't let me breathe," Gaurav muttered, his voice laced with exhaustion and irritation.

"I was thinking... I wish I could land a job in a big company like yours someday," *Chotu* said, almost dreamily.

Gaurav scoffed. "Forget that nonsense. You should focus on growing this stall instead. Private jobs are hell, *Chotu*. Better to be your own boss than be someone's slave."

The cigarette burned between his fingers, but the weight on his chest felt heavier than ever. The pressure, the expectations, the suffocating cycle—it never really ended.

"Is it really that bad in private companies?" *Chotu* asked, curiosity flickering in his voice.

"It's terrible. Some companies are decent, but those are rare," Gaurav replied, shaking his head.

Chotu handed him the tea.

"Your tea is always perfect," Gaurav said, taking a sip, the warmth momentarily soothing his frayed nerves.

But *Chotu* barely reacted. He simply moved on, pouring tea into another cup and handing it to the next customer, like it was just another routine moment in his endless cycle of serving and pouring.

Gaurav watched him for a second—how easily the kid dismissed conversations, how little time he had to bother with words. Maybe he was right. Maybe running this stall was a better life than being stuck in the endless grind of corporate slavery.

Just a few hours ago, Gaurav had been desperate to go home. But now, it was like he didn't care anymore. The frustration had built up—office pressure, family tensions—it was all too much. Balancing both felt like a punishment, an impossible equation he could never solve. He was suffocating under it.

Gaurav thought of his daughter—the tiny cake, the candles, the guests already gathered at home. His heart softened. He exhaled, slipped into the car, and started driving.

He had barely taken a couple of turns when his phone buzzed. A message. From Kundan.

"Tomorrow, you'll find out who you messed with."

Gaurav's jaw tightened. He pulled over to the side and typed a reply, hands shaking slightly: "I've seen plenty like you."

Seconds later, another message flashed on his screen.

"So have I. I've been in the corporate world for 21 years. Guys like you come and go. I'll make a dog out of you—humiliate you in front of the whole office."

Gaurav lost his patience. He dialed Kundan instantly.

Kundan answered.

Before he could get a word in, Gaurav's voice punched through:

"Bol, motherf***er."

There was a short silence. Then a chuckle—mocking, cold. "Oh, trying to be a hero, are you? Just wait. Tomorrow I'll smash that attitude of yours. You think you're special?"

"You've spent 21 years licking boots and bullying interns," Gaurav snapped. "But not this time. You picked the wrong guy."

"Just show up tomorrow," Kundan hissed. "I'll make sure you're thrown out of this job."

Gaurav smiled bitterly. "You won't have to. I resign. Screw your job."

Gaurav ended the call.

The phone went silent, but their tempers didn't. This wasn't just an argument anymore. It was personal.

And tomorrow... the office floor wouldn't just be a workplace—it'd be a battlefield.

Gaurav lit another cigarette, the flame flickering like his frustration. He stood at the edge of the road, exhaling long, angry puffs into the night air, watching the smoke disappear like the patience he'd run out of hours ago.

His head was pounding—not just from exhaustion, but from the chaos spinning in his mind. Kundan's words were still echoing like background noise from a bad movie.

After a few more drags, he felt a slight calm settle in—just enough to think clearly, or maybe just dangerously. He crushed the cigarette under his shoe, walked back to his car, and slid into the seat like a man who had made up his mind.

He opened his laptop. The screen lit up, cold and blue, like an invitation to rebellion.

He began typing:

Hello,

Please accept my resignation.

Thanks & Regards,

Gaurav Rathore

He paused, stared at the words—not with regret, but with a certain fire in his eyes. Then, without blinking, he typed Kundan Jha's name in the "To" field. Added HR and another manager in CC, the kind who nod at every loud voice in the room.

Then came the final move—he clicked Send. A tiny button with the power of a knockout punch.

And just like that, the corporate circus lost one performer who refused to be someone's punching bag. Gaurav didn't wait for applause. He didn't need it.

He started the car, the engine roaring like it shared his urgency. For the first time that evening, he wasn't driving away from something—he was driving towards something that mattered.

It was almost 10 PM when Gaurav reached home.

He rang the doorbell. Ruby opened the door, arms crossed, eyes sharp.

"This is the time you come home? Your daughter's birthday, Gaurav. One day. You could've shown up on time at least today."

"There was pressure at work," Gaurav muttered. "Too much going on. I couldn't finish even half of what was on my plate."

Ruby narrowed her eyes. "Oh really? Work? Or were you with some girl again? You always use that office excuse—you think I'm a fool?"

"Stop this nonsense, Ruby," he snapped. "Your constant suspicion is turning toxic. I'm already suffocating in office politics, and the moment I step home, you serve me this daily dose of drama."

Their voices had risen by now.

Almost all the guests had left. Only Gajendra, Ruby's brother, and Sheetal, her sister-in-law, were still there, finishing up some cake and winding down the evening.

Hearing the commotion, Gajendra stepped forward. *"Bhaiya, bhabhi, bas karo na. Party ka mood aur kharab mat karo,"* he said, placing a gentle hand on Gaurav's shoulder.

Sheetal chimed in softly, "Ruby, it's okay. Let's just end the day peacefully. Tomorrow's another day, *na*?"

Gaurav looked away, jaw tight. Ruby said nothing. The silence that followed wasn't calm—it was just the eye of the storm.

Tiny feet patterned across the living room floor. Khushi came running, cake smeared across her cheeks and joy bouncing in every step. Gaurav bent down with a tired smile, arms open.

"Hello, my sweety. Happy birthday," he whispered, scooping her into his arms.

He wiped the cake gently from her face with his thumb, as if brushing away the stress of the day. For a second, everything else—Kundan's threats, Ruby's anger, the cold war in his inbox—just faded. Khushi giggled and pressed her cheek to his, and Gaurav closed his eyes.

Whatever battles raged outside, this was his real win.

"We'll take your leave now, Gaurav," Gajendra said, getting up and adjusting his watch.

Sheetal gave Ruby a side-hug and smiled softly. "Take care of each other. And please, don't fight over small things. Life's already too messy as it is."

"Gajendra *bhaiya*, you know your sister, right?" Gaurav snapped, unable to hide his irritation. "She'll pick a fight over anything. Office is a mess already, and home isn't any better because of her constant drama."

"Gaurav ji," Sheetal said, raising her hand gently, "a clap takes two hands. If things are falling apart, maybe both of you need to meet halfway. We're outsiders—we can only say 'be happy, live in peace.' But you two... you know what's really going on inside."

The room fell into an awkward silence. Ruby looked away, wounded but stubborn. Gaurav clenched his jaw and nodded.

They walked Gajendra and Sheetal out to the parking area. The chill in the air matched the one between them. As the car disappeared into the street, Gaurav and Ruby stood quietly under the yellow parking lot light—together, but not close.

Sometimes, the worst fights don't end with shouting. They end with silence that says everything.

Gaurav changed out of his work clothes with the kind of detachment that comes after a fight you didn't want to have, but couldn't avoid either. He forced down dinner—just enough so Ruby wouldn't accuse him of skipping meals again—and quietly walked to the bedroom with Khushi in his arms.

Ruby finished the leftover chores—clearing half-eaten plates, picking up crumpled wrappers, and switching off the lights with sharp, loud clicks that said more than words ever could.

Eventually, she came to bed too.

They lay there in silence, backs turned, Khushi in between them like a tiny wall made of love and unfinished sentences.

No more words were exchanged. Just the quiet hum of the ceiling fan and two hearts too tired to argue, too bruised to reach out.

It was one of those nights—heavy, silent, and heartbreakingly still. The kind of night where even sleep feels like a stranger.

CHAPTER TWO

CONFRONTING THE LEADS

Gaurav woke up late. Really late. 9 AM blinked on his phone screen. Even the harsh sunlight filtering through the curtains seemed confused—"How are you still in bed?"

He couldn't remember the last time he'd slept so soundly, despite the emotional wreckage of the night before. He stretched, rubbed his eyes, and the memories of Ruby's sharp words came rushing back like a bad hangover.

They had fought. Again. But then again, what's a marriage without a few battlefield scars? You fight, you patch up, and somehow the circus goes on—especially when there's a kid in the middle of it.

Ruby's voice cut through the silence, laced with sarcasm. "No office today, Mr. I-Have-Deadlines?"

Gaurav glanced at the wall clock and muttered, "I'll go a bit late today."

Of course, he didn't tell her the real reason. That he might be going to the office for the **last** time. That after the ugly showdown with Kundan last night, anything could happen today. Better to let the tea flow and the storm wait.

"Give me some tea. I'll bathe and head out," he said, as he sat beside Khushi, gently running his fingers through her hair. "She's still asleep. Let her rest—she stayed up late last night."

There was calm on the surface. But inside him, a hundred drums were beating.

By 10:15, he stepped out of the house, dressed sharply—but there was an unfamiliar chill in the air. His body was walking toward the office, but his mind kept flashing back to Kundan's messages and threats: "***Main tujhe zillat ka tamasha banaunga.(I will make you a spectacle of humiliation)***"

He stopped by the local tea stall outside his office building—the one with the rusty tin roof and over-sweet tea that somehow still hit better than Starbucks.

"*Ek kadak dena, Chotu*," he said to the *chaiwala*, then pulled out his phone and scrolled to Kapil's number.

Kapil, his oldest friend in the office. The one who knew where all the skeletons were buried.

"Hello?" Kapil said.

"Bhai, I sent the mail last night," Gaurav said, taking a sip. "Resignation done. I'm not going to sit and take Kundan's shit anymore."

Gaurav recounted everything that had happened the previous day.

Kapil was silent for a second. Then he exhaled. "*Tu pagla gaya hai. Tu jaanta bhi hai aaj kya hoga?(Have you gone mad? Do you even know what's going to happen)*"

"I don't care," Gaurav said calmly. "Let him rage. Let them gossip. I'm done dancing in someone else's circus."

"Where are you right now?" Kapil asked.

"At *Chotu's* tea stall. Where are you?"

"I'm in the office. I'll come there."

Within a few minutes, Kapil arrived at the stall. Both of them greeted each other with a simple "hey."

Just then, a bullet bike pulled up near them. A guy and a girl got off—Sunny and Yogita. Both worked in the same company. Both of them were late for office today. But like always, they stopped at the same tea stall before stepping inside the building.

Yogita carried a soft fullness in her frame—neither too heavy nor too light, just enough to give her presence a comforting warmth. But her face told a different story; the constant pressure of work etched subtle lines of worry across her forehead. Even when she smiled, there was a lingering tiredness in her eyes, as if she was carrying more than just her own burdens.

"Hey, Sunny!" Gaurav greeted, shaking his hand. Sunny was a mystery—a man who loved uncovering secrets but never revealed his own.

Sunny Chaudhari wasn't in the company because of his talent. Let's get that straight.

He had a political background—someone powerful had dropped his name during hiring, and just like that, he landed a seat in the tech team. Coding? He couldn't tell Java from Javascript. But this is India, right? If you have the right connections, even a donkey can get a job and be served tea like a CEO. Sunny was one of those donkeys—only louder.

He was a bit... off. The kind of guy who brought Parliament debates to lunch breaks and thought every office conflict was part of some political conspiracy.

Lately, he had developed a sudden interest in Yogita. Flirting in the corridors, lingering a little too long at her desk, offering chai like he was the male lead of a B-grade college romance. A few weeks ago, he had tried the same with someone else—different name, same failed script.

Yogita, thankfully, had better taste.

"Hi Yogita," Gaurav said with a strong handshake.

Kapil greeted them too, passing a cigarette to Sunny.

The four of them—good friends, bound by the shared misery of their workplace.

Gaurav handed tea cups to Sunny and Yogita and ordered two more.

"So, how's life treating you, Yogita?" Gaurav asked.

She let out a tired sigh. "What do I even say? My situation is as bad as yours. Kundan assigned me a project with a deadline for next week. He asks for updates twice a day—once in the morning and then again just before leaving. Honestly, sometimes I feel like just not showing up at the office. But then, I have no choice."

"What do you mean, no choice? You're single—you don't have family responsibilities. What expenses do you even have?" Gaurav asked, puzzled.

"It looks easy from the outside," Yogita said, shaking her head. "Only I know how things are at home. That's why I left Himachal to roast in this Delhi-NCR heat."

"Don't stress so much. Have this fan. You probably didn't even have breakfast," Gaurav said, handing her the snack.

Yogita smirked at Sunny. "See? This is what you call a caring man."

Sunny grinned. "Yeah, yeah, I see that. But why's he acting so cheerful today? Kundan has screwed him over too."

Before Gaurav could answer, Kapil jumped in.

"He resigned. Sent his resignation email last night. That's why he's glowing today," Kapil said with a chuckle.

"What?!" Yogita exclaimed, stunned, nearly choking on the fan. She quickly wiped her mouth with a napkin. "Are you serious, Gaurav?"

"Hmm," Gaurav nodded casually, sipping his tea.

"Where's your next job?" Sunny asked.

"Nowhere yet. Just quit this one. I'll figure it out," Gaurav replied, unfazed.

"But why?" Sunny frowned.

"You know how bad it's been, bro. This company has been sucking the life out of us. Just ask Yogita—look at how stressed she is. She's gaining weight just from the pressure. Where do you think all this stress is coming from? This damn company." Gaurav said, placing his empty cup aside.

"What tension do you have, Sunny?" Gaurav said, teasing him. "You've got a direct setting with the manager—no worries about increment, no stress about promotion, and absolutely zero tension about work."

Sunny had to accept reality. And eventually, even he started enjoying the joke himself.

"How much is it, *Chotu*?" Gaurav asked.

"120," *Chotu* replied.

Gaurav tapped his phone and paid the bill. Then he turned to Yogita with a smile. "Lunch is on me today. All of you. No arguments."

Kapil already knew what was going on. He was well aware that Gaurav had only sent in his resignation—no one had accepted it yet. To him, it felt like Gaurav was celebrating a little too early.

Still, he was a good friend. So, with a smirk, he said, "First go have a chat with Amrish Puri—yes, the villain from those old movies. Our very own boss. Let's see if he even lets you go. You barely wrapped up one part of his project yesterday. Five modules are still hanging."

Gaurav scoffed and stood up. "That clown? He can't stop me."

He took one last drag from his cigarette, crushed it beneath his foot, and gestured towards the office.

"Let's go," he said.

Gaurav barely had time to settle at his desk when HR Drishti appeared beside him.

"Gaurav, can you please come to the conference room with me?" Her tone was formal, but her eyes held the kind of tension you'd see before a bomb squad moved in.

"Sure, ma'am," he replied coolly, picking up his notepad even though he knew he wouldn't need it.

As they entered the conference room, Gaurav immediately spotted Kundan—arms folded, nostrils flaring like an angry bull—and Vipul Bajaj, the General Manager, seated with a stern face that looked permanently stuck in 'disappointed principal' mode.

Kundan had insisted on this closed-door meeting. He didn't want a public scene. He knew Gaurav was capable of tearing him apart, word by word, in front of the entire office. So he played safe—controlled environment, HR present, GM watching.

But Kundan couldn't hide his rage. He said, "What the hell do you think you're doing, Gaurav?" he barked. "How dare you talk to me yesterday? This isn't your father's company!"

Gaurav's eyes didn't flinch. "No, it's not my father's company. But thank God for that—because if it were, I would fire you in the first place."

Vipul shifted in his seat. Drishti looked like she wanted to be anywhere else.

Kundan slammed his palm on the table. "*Tameez se baat kar.* You have no idea what I can do. One word from me and no one in this industry will hire you again!"

Gaurav leaned forward, voice steady, but sharp as a blade. "Do it. Blacklist me. Threaten me. Go ahead. But remember—your power only works on people who need you. I don't. You're twenty years into this game, Kundan... and still insecure about your job."

"You're crossing the line, Gaurav!"

Vipul interrupted both of them.

HR cleared her throat and leaned forward. "Gaurav, we received your resignation email at 10 PM . What's going on? Why do you want to leave?"

Silence.

Vipul Bajaj joined in, "Speak up, Gaurav. If something's wrong, tell us. Why did you make this decision?"

Gaurav's face hardened. His jaw clenched. "Sir, because of this man." He pointed straight at Kundan. "Either fire him or accept my resignation."

The room fell silent . A wave of shock passed through everyone.

"Gaurav, Mr. Kundan has been working here for 21 years . No one has ever raised a complaint against him," HR Drishti said, trying to keep his tone neutral.

Gaurav let out a dry laugh. "No one speaks up to his face. That's the problem. But behind his back? Everyone curses him. " His gaze was locked on Kundan, unflinching.

Vipul Bajaj, the senior manager, stepped in like the school principal breaking up a playground fight. He raised both hands and said firmly, "Enough. This isn't how professionals behave."

He looked at Kundan, then at Gaurav. "We all have egos, but let's not forget—we're here to build, not break." His voice was calm, but carried weight.

With effort, and a bit of awkwardness, he got both of them to shake hands. It wasn't warm, but it was a handshake.

"For the sake of the company," Vipul added, "I expect you both to move forward from here. Work together. Think of the bigger picture."

Then he turned to Gaurav. "You can head back to your seat now."

Gaurav gave a stiff nod, pushed the door open, and walked out. The conference room drama was done—but in his head, the final act was still being written.

For the next five minutes , HR, the senior manager , and Kundan had a private discussion.

Gaurav had just opened his laptop when a new email notification popped up .

"Resignation accepted. You have to serve a 2-month **notice period** starting today."

It was from HR.

Gaurav smirked slightly. He typed a simple reply — "Thanks."

And then, another mail arrived—from Kundan.

"These are 15 corrections that need to be fixed ASAP. Please provide me with a time estimation. These are the corrections from your last work which you delivered yesterday."

Without even reading the full email , Gaurav typed back— "It will take approx. 25 to 30 days."

Kundan saw the reply but didn't argue. He knew the task would barely take 10-15 days . But after that confrontation in the meeting room, he wasn't about to challenge Gaurav further.

If Gaurav lashed out publicly , it would humiliate him. And Kundan had no intention of letting that happen.

A few seats away, Gaurav caught Kapil's eye and made a subtle gesture— smoke break.

They headed to the terrace of the office building.

Gaurav lit his cigarette, took a deep drag, then passed it to Kapil.

"Bro, they accepted my resignation ," he said, blowing out smoke.

"What?! Kundan didn't stop you? " Kapil asked, surprised.

"Oh, everyone tried. But I told them— either Kundan stays, or I do. "

"And?"

"What do you think?" Gaurav smirked. " He's been here for 21 years. They chose him. And just like that, HR sent me the confirmation email—'Resignation accepted.' "

"And Kundan? He didn't say anything?"

"You should've seen his face. He looked completely crushed. All that arrogance— gone . He just sent me a mail about corrections. I told him for one month . He knows it won't take that long, but he won't argue. And who knows? Maybe I'll stretch this task to the full two months. "

They both laughed.

Then, finishing their cigarettes, they walked back inside, ready for whatever came next.

In the afternoon, the cafeteria buzzed with chatter, but at one table, the energy was different. Loud. Happy. Carefree. Gaurav was in a rare mood—grinning like a man who had just won his freedom, laughing like there were no worries left in his life.

"Eat whatever you want. Drink whatever you want. It's all on me today!" he declared, tapping the table, making heads turn around them.

"You sure, boss?" Sunny asked, raising an eyebrow.

"I just quit the worst job of my life. If this isn't a celebration moment, what is?" Gaurav laughed, signaling the waiter. *"Bhaiya, ek ek butter naan aur lagao Aur paneer bhi! Full party mood mein hain aaj!"*

Kapil chuckled, shaking his head. "Gaurav, a week ago, you were talking about EMIs, responsibilities, and life struggles. And today?"

"Today, I'm free." Gaurav took a bite of paneer, exaggerating his enjoyment. "Mmm. This is what freedom tastes like."

Yogita smiled, taking a sip of her cold drink. "Honestly, I envy your confidence. If I resigned, I'd be panicking already."

"That's because you think too much," Gaurav pointed out. "See, you don't need a perfect plan. Just trust that you'll figure it out. And meanwhile..." He leaned forward, grabbing a gulab jamun, "...enjoy the sweetness."

Sunny laughed, "You sound like some *baba* giving life lessons."

"Baba Rathore!" Kapil teased, and the whole table erupted in laughter.

For the first time in months, the office stress, the deadlines, the suffocating pressure—it all seemed far away.

And for today, that was enough.

Gaurav had no idea how fast the day had flown by.

One moment, he was laughing at lunch with his friends, the next, he was catching up with people he hadn't spoken to in months. He called his mother, who lived in the village, then dialed an old friend, then his brother—just relishing the freedom of the day, the feeling of being in control again.

As the evening approached, he didn't drag his work like usual.

At exactly 6:55 PM, he shut down his laptop—no overthinking, no last-minute replies, no stress. He packed up, stretched a little, and got ready to leave.

Before stepping out, he met Kapil, Sunny, and Yogita, exchanging a few jokes, grinning ear to ear, like this was the start of something new.

Then, with a casual wave, he walked out of the office doors—for the first time in years, feeling light.

Before starting his car, Gaurav dialed Ruby's number.

"Hello," she answered, her tone indifferent.

"I just left the office. Need me to pick up anything?" Gaurav asked, keeping his voice calm.

"Oh, now you remember home? Calling after an entire day?" Ruby snapped.

"Let's not argue over the phone. I'm on my way home—we'll talk then. Just tell me if you need anything."

"No," she said curtly, and hung up.

Gaurav sighed, slipping his phone into his bag and starting the car. His mind whirled with thoughts—work was settled, but now, he had to fix things at home.

After about an hour, he reached home and rang the bell.

Ruby opened the door.

She froze. Surprised. Confused.

On one hand, Gaurav held bags full of groceries, chocolates, and scented candles. A delivery guy beside him was carrying a full-size pink teddy bear—a gift for his three-year-old daughter.

But that wasn't all.

Behind the teddy, he pulled out a tiny princess dress, a pair of sparkling shoes, and a soft bedtime storybook—things to make his little one giggle with joy.

For Ruby, he had bought her favorite perfume, a delicate bracelet, and a box of luxury chocolates.

Ruby's expression softened—just slightly.

"Peace offering?" she asked, crossing her arms.

"Call it whatever you want," Gaurav smirked. "Now, are you letting me in, or do I stand here with this giant teddy all night?"

Gaurav stepped inside, placing the bags down, and without a second thought, pulled Ruby into a tight hug.

She hesitated for a moment, then sighed—like she was letting go of some of her anger, just a little.

Without saying a word, Gaurav moved towards the other room.

There she was—his little princess, sitting on the floor, playing with her toys.

The moment she saw him, her tiny eyes lit up.

"Papa!" she squealed, running towards him, arms wide.

Gaurav scooped her up, showering kisses on her soft cheeks, his heart full.

He had quit his job. He had walked away from the stress. And now—this was the only thing that mattered.

He closed his eyes for a second, taking in the moment.

"Papa brought you something!" he said, holding up the big pink teddy bear.

Her squeal of pure excitement filled the room.

"What's for dinner?" Gaurav asked, stretching a little.

"I haven't cooked anything yet," Ruby replied casually.

"Good! You did the right thing," Gaurav smirked. "I ordered your favorite pizza ten minutes ago—along with cold drinks. No need to cook tonight."

Ruby couldn't help but smile.

Gaurav kicked off his shoes, headed to the washroom, and freshened up. By the time he was back, the pizza had arrived.

As they ate, the conversation drifted to Khushi's birthday yesterday. Ruby was still a little upset—probably about something Gaurav forgot—but the pizza, the cold drinks, and her favorite chocolates were working their magic.

"Listen... let's go somewhere tomorrow," Gaurav suggested, bouncing Khushi lightly in his arms. She was curled up against him, drinking milk from her bottle.

"You have office tomorrow, don't you?" Ruby asked.

"Yeah, but I'll take a sick leave."

Ruby thought for a moment. "Then let's go to a water park. Khushi will enjoy it."

"Done. Look up the best water park in Delhi NCR, and we'll go there."

"Starting this Saturday, I'm going to play cricket again. It's a childhood hobby I've really missed. But not anymore—I'm bringing it back."

"Ok. If you find time, then I don't have any issue."

Their conversation continued late into the night—light-hearted, easy, almost like old times.

As soon as Khushi fell asleep, Gaurav nudged Ruby's hand softly, gesturing towards the other room.

Ruby lifted her head slightly, whispering, "What happened?"

Gaurav simply winked and kissed her lightly.

Ruby understood immediately—a small smile playing on her lips. Silently, they slipped out of the room, careful not to wake their daughter.

In the dim glow of the bedside lamp, Ruby leaned against the wall, arms crossed, eyes playful.

"You're being secretive tonight," she murmured.

Gaurav grinned. "I just realized I haven't stolen a moment like this in ages."

He traced a finger down her wrist, slowly pulling her toward him. The space between them faded—warm, familiar, intoxicating.

For a few seconds, neither of them spoke.

There was no rush. No deadlines. No work stress hanging over them. Just this moment, where they could finally be them, without the weight of everything else.

Ruby sighed, resting her forehead against his chest.

Gaurav ran his fingers through her hair, gently, taking in her presence, her warmth, her scent.

She looked up, searching his face.

He kissed her—slow, deep, unhurried. A kiss that said everything he hadn't been able to say in months.

Ruby melted into him.

They lay down, tangled in each other, breathing in sync, their bodies warm against the cool sheets.

Both were lost in their private, intense moments.

CHAPTER THREE

MOMENTS THAT MATTER

"Good morning," Ruby said, her voice carrying a hint of happiness—like last night had been magical, like she was silently thanking Gaurav for it.

"Good morning," Gaurav replied, lazily adjusting the pillow against the wall and reclining halfway, settling in comfortably.

Ruby placed the steaming cup of tea on the bedside table.

Beside him, Khushi lay curled up, still in her little dream world. Gaurav gently ran his hand over her tiny back, feeling the softness of her presence, the innocence of her sleep.

"When did you wake up?" he asked.

"An hour ago. I even took a shower," Ruby replied, sipping her tea.

Gaurav smirked. "Why? We're going to a water park, right? You're gonna get drenched anyway."

Ruby rolled her eyes. "Idiot. We go to a water park for fun activities—not for a bath. We get wet, sure, but it's not like you grab soap and start scrubbing yourself there!"

Gaurav laughed at her dramatic tone. "Fine, fine. I'll take a shower too, then we'll go."

"Relax, we don't leave this early. Water parks are fun around noon. Let me make breakfast first."

Just as she was about to get up, Gaurav caught her wrist and pulled her toward him.

"Breakfast will happen, but first, come here for a second."

Ruby sighed, giving him a look, but settled beside him anyway.

"So, tell me—what if I quit this job completely?" he asked, sounding serious.

Ruby frowned. "Absolutely not. How will we manage expenses? And why are you talking about this first thing in the morning?"

"Sorry, sorry. Just messing with you." Gaurav chuckled, leaning in to plant a quick kiss on her cheek.

"Drink your tea. I'm going to the kitchen," Ruby said, shaking her head, but there was a small smile playing on her lips.

A few minutes later, Gaurav finished his tea and flipped open his laptop.

He typed out a single, effortless email to his office:

"Not feeling well today. Taking sick leave."

No request. No explanation. Just a statement—as if declaring his own rules now.

Gaurav stepped out of the shower and headed straight to the kitchen.

"Need me to do anything?" he asked, just as his eyes landed on Khushi, sitting on the kitchen floor, playing with her toys. He smiled and scooped her up into his arms.

"You cook the vegetables, I'll bathe Khushi," Ruby said.

"No, no! Today, I'll do it. Let's see if she enjoys it."

Ruby raised an eyebrow. "It's not as easy as you think. But fine, go ahead—I'll watch and guide you."

A few minutes later, they were all in the bathroom.

Gaurav gently bathed Khushi, following Ruby's instructions. At one point, he let her sit in the bathtub, splashing around, giggling.

"Don't keep her in for too long," Ruby reminded him. "She might have caught a cold."

Gaurav nodded and picked her up, wrapping her in a towel. Together, he and Ruby dressed her in soft, comfy clothes, making her look even more adorable.

After a few moments, Gaurav stood in front of the mirror, running his fingers through his hair. But his eyes lingered on his reflection.

His physique had changed.

His once-defined biceps—a reminder of his old gym routine—had lost their sharpness. His shoulders, still broad, didn't have the same edge they once did. Work stress, long office hours, and neglect had taken a toll.

"Ruby, I'm starting the morning gym tomorrow," he declared.

"You barely have time in the mornings. How will you manage?" Ruby asked.

"Earlier, I had to reach by 9 sharp. Now, I'll go in by 10."

"Why the sudden change?"

"That project's done—the one keeping me under pressure," he lied. He still hadn't told Ruby about his resignation.

"Fine, go if you want. I don't care," Ruby muttered, making a face. "But pick a gym where only guys go. No girls. I know how men are—always checking them out."

Gaurav rolled his eyes. "Keep this nonsense to yourself, Ruby. I'm just going to talk to the gym owner, that's it."

"Have breakfast first," Ruby suggested.

"You make it—I'll be back in five minutes. Taking Khushi with me."

Ruby nodded, heading to the kitchen, while Gaurav carried Khushi out, lost in thought.

After a short while, Gaurav returned after talking to the gym owner.

Ruby was also ready for the Water Park.

Gaurav put on a t-shirt and trousers, and within moments, everyone was ready to go.

The sun was high, and the excitement was tangible. After a smooth 30-minute drive, Gaurav parked the car, stretched a little, and led Ruby and Khushi toward the entrance of the water park. He bought the tickets, and soon, they were inside, surrounded by the sound of splashing water and excited chatter from other visitors.

Their first stop was the wave pool, where artificial waves crashed, mimicking the ocean's thrill.

Gaurav held Khushi tightly, letting her tiny feet dangle in the water. The first wave hit, lifting them slightly, making her burst into giggles. Ruby, standing beside them, splashed water toward Khushi, making her squeal louder.

Gaurav laughed. "She's loving it!"

Khushi, barely able to form full sentences, clapped her little hands, shouting in excitement every time a wave rolled over them.

Next were the twin water slides, twisting their way down into a massive splash pool.

Gaurav grinned at Ruby. "Let's go. This one's ours."

"No way. You go," Ruby protested, shaking her head.

"Come on. For old times' sake."

She sighed but gave in. Holding hands, they zoomed down together, the rush of water, the free-fall, the laughter—pure, unfiltered joy. As they crashed into the pool below, Ruby screamed, half from thrill, half from shock, and Gaurav roared with laughter, pulling her close.

Khushi stood at the edge, watching wide-eyed, clapping and pointing as if telling them to do it again.

Just as they were enjoying themselves, Gaurav noticed something off—a man near the pool with a camera, clicking pictures.

Suspicious, he walked over. "Oye, what are you doing? Show me."

The man hesitated. Gaurav's voice was firm, his presence commanding.

The guy tried stepping back, but Gaurav grabbed the camera.

And then—rage.

Among the photos was one of Ruby—her wet clothes clinging to her, her body clearly visible in a way it shouldn't be.

In one swift motion, he smashed the camera against the ground.

"You disgusting—"

Before he could finish, the man shoved him, but Gaurav didn't flinch.

One punch. Straight to the jaw.

The man staggered back, dazed, but lunged at Gaurav again.

Wrong move.

Gaurav dodged, grabbed his collar, and slammed him into the railing.

It was over in seconds.

Security rushed in, pulling the guy away. Ruby looked shaken, but grateful.

Gaurav wrapped an arm around her, pressing a soft kiss to her forehead. "Forget him. Let's get back to having fun."

She exhaled, nodded. "Yeah, let's."

And just like that, they walked away—leaving behind the broken camera, a bruised coward, and a lesson no one would forget.

After hours of splashing in the water, licking ice creams, stuffing themselves with golgappas and greasy junk food, the exhaustion finally kicked in.

They settled into the car, heading home, feeling equal parts tired and satisfied.

Ruby leaned back, watching the road as Gaurav drove.

"Tell me something," she said suddenly. "Weren't you scared? Smashing his camera, fighting him?"

Gaurav smirked, eyes still on the road. "Guess you don't know much about my past."

Ruby raised an eyebrow. "Wait—what? Were you some short-tempered fighter back then?"

"Not a fighter. But definitely not the calm guy I've been for the last 4 - 5 years."

Ruby was intrigued now. "Okay, tell me. What were you like before?"

Gaurav grinned. "Let's do this—I'll grab a few beers, we'll have a mini party at home, and I'll tell you everything."

"No alcohol, please," Ruby sighed.

Gaurav chuckled. "How long has it been since I last asked for beer?"

Ruby thought for a second, unable to recall.

"See? You don't even remember. It's not like I drink every day! Once or twice a month is fine, and this time, it's been a whole six months."

She hesitated, then finally sighed. "Fine."

Gaurav smiled, knowing that his change in behavior was the real reason she was agreeing.

He pulled over at a liquor store, grabbed three beers, then stopped at a nearby shop to get popcorn for Ruby, Fruity for Khushi, and some peanuts for himself.

This was the first time that when they had left home, it was for the excitement of the water park.

And now, as they headed back, the excitement had shifted.

Gaurav was pumped for his mini party, already planning the beer.

Ruby, on the other hand, was eager for something else—to finally hear about the past Gaurav had never spoken about.

A few minutes later, they were home.

It was 8 PM now.

Khushi, exhausted from all the fun, had fallen asleep. Ruby gently fed her milk, tucking her in for the night.

Meanwhile, Gaurav had stretched himself out on the sofa, legs sprawled, back comfortably resting against the cushions. A beer can sat beside him, already open, as he took slow, lazy sips, letting the chilled liquid calm his senses.

Just then, his phone rang.

It was Yogita.

"Hi, Yogita," Gaurav answered, picking up.

"Hello, Gaurav! How are you?" her voice sounded tired.

"I'm good. What about you?"

"What do I even say, yaar? Terrible. Work, work, and more work. Kundan didn't let me leave earlier, and I've just stepped out of the office now. He told me to come on Saturday and Sunday too."

"Seriously?"

"Yes. By the way, I called you because next week's my birthday, and I'm hosting a small party at my place. You HAVE to come, okay?"

"Done. See you at the office on Monday—I'll plan something special for your birthday."

"Great! Bye."

The call ended.

A few seconds later, Ruby walked into the hall, settling beside Gaurav, her legs tucked comfortably beneath her as she leaned against the sofa. She grabbed her cold drink, took a sip, and looked at him.

Gaurav glanced at her sideways, smirking. "Finally done putting Khushi to sleep?"

Ruby sighed, shaking her head. "You should've seen how much she tossed and turned."

Gaurav chuckled and took another sip of his beer.

Ruby asked, her tone casual but with an unmistakable sharpness. "I was listening to a girl's voice. Who was she on the call? Don't tell me you've got some secret office affair going on."

Gaurav didn't even look up from his phone. "Ruby, this habit of doubting everything needs to stop. I'm sensible enough to know that cheating on your wife isn't just wrong—it's against everything I believe in."

There was a pause. Ruby clicked her tongue and looked away. "Relax. I was just joking."

But she wasn't, not entirely. Doubt wasn't new to Ruby—it had become second nature. Like a reflex. She wanted to trust him, but somewhere, that little voice always whispered, what if...?

Ruby sat up straight, looking at Gaurav with curiosity. "Forget that. Now tell me—what was your past like? What kind of person were you?"

For now, it was just the two of them, the night stretching lazily ahead, with nothing to rush, nowhere to go—just peace.

Gaurav placed his beer aside, took a deep breath, and said, "Alright. But before I get into it, I need to remind you of something that happened two months ago. Do you remember when we were on our way to the hospital to get Khushi's injection, and suddenly, a cow appeared in front of our car on the road?"

Ruby nodded. "Yeah, I remember."

Gaurav continued, "Because of the cow, I had to hit the brakes instantly. And that's when the car behind us crashed into our car from the back."

Ruby smirked. "Oh yes, and then the driver got out and slapped you."

Gaurav sighed. "What do you think—whose fault was it?"

"I don't know," Ruby shrugged. "But I do remember that you got slapped." She laughed, teasing him.

"It was his fault. He was driving too close, and when I hit the brakes, he couldn't stop in time. The mistake was his, but I still ended up getting slapped. I'm bringing this up because this is who I am now. But a few years ago, during college—I was different. Very different."

*****

#Five Years Ago – College Days#

The college was buzzing with nervous energy. Today was a practical day, and the examiner was from another college—which meant no chances, no leniency.

Everyone had been called in at sharp 7 AM.

The students had arrived, tension in the air, minds focused on the experiments ahead.

Except for one person.

Gaurav hadn't shown up yet.

PBS Engineering College, Uttar Pradesh. Final year of B.Tech.

These mid-term practicals held serious weight—marks that could shape futures.

The clock hit 7:30 AM, and Gaurav finally entered the lab, hurried but composed.

The subject? Durgesh Pandey's class. The man had a reputation—strict, unforgiving, feared. And today, he was in charge.

The moment Pandey sir spotted Gaurav, his face twisted in rage.

"Gaurav! Come here—right now!" he thundered.

"Yes, sir," Gaurav responded, stepping forward.

"Is this the time to arrive? 7 AM was the practical time. The practical has already started!"

"Sir, my car got punctured on the way, that's why I got delayed. Give me the sheet—I'll catch up."

Pandey sir let out a sharp laugh, dripping with sarcasm.

"Oh, listen to him! Talking as if he knows everything, as if he's the class topper!"

"Sir, if I fail, that's my loss. If I waste the year, it's on me. Why are you getting so worked up?"

Pandey sir's face darkened. "Your failure ruins MY results!"

And before anyone could react, he slapped Gaurav—hard, furious, unforgiving.

For a second, silence.

Then? Chaos.

Gaurav didn't even hesitate. His fists swung instinctively, landing 3–4 solid punches straight at Pandey sir, knocking him off balance. A kick followed, and suddenly—the strictest professor in college was on the ground.

Gasps filled the room. Students stood frozen, watching in shock.

A few rushed in, pulling Gaurav away, trying to calm him down.

Breathing heavy, anger still burning, Gaurav locked eyes with Pandey sir, who staggered up, humiliated, speechless.

Without a word, Pandey sir turned and marched straight to the Dean's office.

The incident spread like wildfire. Word traveled across the campus—Gaurav had just knocked out Pandey sir.

Because of the chaos, the practical was postponed, and soon enough—Gaurav was summoned to the Dean's room.

Gaurav walked into the dean's office with his usual swagger. "Good that you called me, sir. Otherwise, I was coming to see you anyway," he said, settling into the chair without waiting for permission.

The dean ignored his casual tone and cut straight to the point. "How dare you raise your hand against Mr. Pandey? Do students hit their teachers?" His voice was sharp, laced with anger.

Gaurav leaned forward, his expression darkening. "Sir, that's exactly my question—how could Pandey sir hit me first? This isn't some primary school where teachers can punish students like kids. This is a professional course. Here, we don't have a 'teacher-student' relationship. It's purely professional. A teacher comes, delivers a lecture, and leaves. That's it." He paused for a moment, measuring his words. "Pandey sir needs to be removed. He cannot teach our class anymore. Find another professor. Anyone, but not him. If that doesn't happen..." He let the sentence hang in the air before adding, "Pandey sir knows me well enough to understand what I'll do next."

The dean narrowed his eyes. "Are you threatening me?"

"Sir, Pandey sir was wrong. He should be punished, not me," Gaurav said firmly.

The dean turned to the peon. "Check the records for Gaurav's father's number."

Gaurav leaned back with a smirk. "No need to check records. I'll give you the number. Note it down." He started dictating the digits, his voice unwavering.

The dean punched the numbers into his phone, waited a second, then said, "Hello, Mr. Rathore. This is the dean speaking."

"Hello, sir. What a surprise! What made you call?" Gaurav's father answered casually.

The dean wasted no time and narrated the entire incident.

"My son is right. I trust him completely, and he has my full permission to handle this situation however he sees fit," Mr. Rathore said, his tone firm and unwavering. "I suggest you explain to your professors that such behavior is unacceptable."

The dean sighed and hung up the phone.

"Well, that's sorted then. I'll take my leave now, sir," Gaurav said, getting up. "But let's be clear—Mr. Pandey will no longer be teaching our class." And with that, he walked out.

For the next few days, another professor took over Pandey's lectures. But the damage had already been done. Word spread like wildfire through the college—everyone knew what had happened. The humiliation was too much. In the end, Durgesh Pandey himself resigned and joined another institution.

Gaurav's fearless attitude was legendary in college. Everyone knew that when his Bullet roared through the campus, it wasn't just the sound—it was a statement. Yet, despite his tough persona, he was fiercely loyal to his friends, always ready for a good time.

*****

Gaurav took a long sip of his beer, tossed a few peanuts into his mouth, and leaned back. "Now I get it... the way I used to be. Smashing that camera at the water park and beating up that guy—it made me realize something. I miss that version of myself. I think I want to be that guy again."

Ruby raised an eyebrow. "You literally challenged Pandey sir in front of the dean. That was insane!"

Gaurav smirked. "That was just one episode. There are plenty more where that came from." He paused, gauging her reaction. "But don't ask me to spill all of them now. Someday, when I feel like it, I'll tell you more."

Ruby shook her head in disbelief. "OMG! I always thought you were timid, a quiet, non-confrontational guy. But you were fearless!"

Gaurav stretched his arms. "Listen, I'm starving. Either order something, or get up and make something right now."

"You enjoy your beer. I'll whip up something in ten minutes," Ruby said, heading toward the kitchen. In a few minutes, she gave him salted boiled corn.

Gaurav finished his beer and strolled into the kitchen. Ruby was rolling out rotis, completely absorbed in her task. Without warning, he wrapped his arms around her from behind. His grip was lazy, the slight buzz from the alcohol making him lean into her a little more than necessary.

"Someone's been extra romantic these days," Ruby said, glancing sideways but not stopping her work.

"Hmm, we eat first, then maybe... some *shanky-panky*?" Gaurav teased, nudging her playfully.

Ruby laughed, shaking her head. "Shut up," she said in a tone that wasn't entirely dismissive, more like she was enjoying the banter but pretending to protest.

Today was just like yesterday—filled with happiness, laughter, and the kind of moments that make life feel light and effortless. The night, too, carried the same warmth, like a continuation of the joy that refused to fade away.

CHAPTER FOUR

HEART KNEW WHERE TO STAY

"I'm going to play cricket. I've joined a club. They have matches every Saturday, and on weekdays, we can go for practice in the evenings if we coordinate," Gaurav told Ruby as he packed his kit bag.

Ruby frowned. "There's so much work to do at home, and all you care about is playing cricket?" she said.

Gaurav didn't even look up. He slung his cricket bag over his shoulder. "I already told you about my hobby and about cricket."

Without waiting for a response, he walked out.

Four kilometers away, he reached a cricket stadium. The place felt alive—the distant echoes of batting practice, the rhythmic thud of balls hitting the turf. Cricket had been his love since childhood. And now, finally, he was actively involved. He met his teammates and got started with practice.

Meanwhile, in the office, Yogita sat alone. Everyone else had Saturday off, but thanks to Kundan's pressure, she had to show up.

She hated it. Hated that she was the only one from her team stuck here. She leaned back in her chair, annoyed at herself for not saying no.

Needing some relief, she called Gaurav.

"Hi, Gaurav," she said.

"Hello. Your voice sounds dull. Everything okay?" Gaurav asked, wiping sweat off his face with a towel.

"Yeah, I'm stuck in the office. Kundan gave a Monday deadline for this project."

"Oh, office. Who else is around?" Gaurav sat down on the stadium steps.

"Seven or eight people, but they're sitting scattered on the floor. None from our department. Sunny's here too, but you know I don't like to talk to him."

Gaurav smiled faintly. "Yeah, I know."

"Sunny's two rows away," she added.

"Alright. Get your work done. I'm heading back to practice."

"Talk to me a little longer. I'm feeling awful in the office. There's no one here."

"Come on, don't be so sad. You did this to yourself. You should've clearly told Kundan you weren't coming to the office on Saturday. Now that you're here, just finish your work."

"You're enjoying your Saturday way too much..."

"Hmm, you could come too. We'll treat you."

"Shut up, Gaurav. I've gained so much weight. If I start running on the ground, people will get scared and say an elephant calf is on the loose."

"*Haha*, yeah, you have put on some weight. Maybe take care of your health before it gets worse."

"If I ever get free from office work, then I'll think about my body... Anyway, where do you play?"

"Patel Nagar. There's this stadium nearby—OPR Stadium. We play there. Today's my first day."

"Okay, nice. Are you coming to the office on Monday?"

"Not fixed. If there's nothing else priority-wise, I'll come."

"Alright."

"So, we're done with the chit-chat? Can I go play now?"

"No."

"What?"

"Hmm. No. Talk to me."

"There's nothing left to talk about. You're just killing time now. If you really want to talk, come here. Bye bye, I'm hanging up now. My team's waiting."

"Okay, bye bye. Go play."

Yogita hung up.

She sat still for a while, as if nothing made sense anymore. But she didn't look tense. They say when you do things that bring you happiness, your brain releases dopamine, which lifts your mood. Talking to Gaurav had done the same for her—something about his cool, calm voice, his grounded presence. It made her feel lighter.

She shut her laptop and packed it inside her bag.

A few minutes later, she was out of the office, the bag slung over her shoulder, stepping into the world outside.

Gaurav was completely lost in the game.

He didn't know everyone on the field, but he had already connected with two players—Sidhu, his neighbor, and Sanju. Within a single day, Sanju had also become his cricket buddy, sharing laughs and strategizing between overs.

"Sanju, stop swinging like a drunk swordsman. Keep your head steady, watch the ball till the last second," Gaurav said, adjusting his gloves.

Sidhu grinned. "Sanju plays like he's in a hurry to catch a train."

"Exactly. And Sidhu, your cover drive is solid, but you're losing balance while playing it. Adjust your footwork a little, stay firm on the crease," Gaurav advised, patting him on the shoulder.

Sanju leaned against his bat, catching his breath. "This pitch is slow, man. The ball's not coming on to the bat."

"Then stop going for flashy strokes. Place the ball in gaps, take twos and threes," Gaurav said, calm as ever.

Sidhu sighed. "I keep mistiming my pull shots."

"That's because you're playing too early. Wait for the ball, let it come to you. Timing is everything," Gaurav explained, stretching his arms.

Sidhu smirked. "Alright, coach. Let's put your wisdom to the test."

Gaurav chuckled. "You'll thank me when you smash your first boundary."

With that, the game resumed. Gaurav was giving coaching to guys.

It had been almost an hour of practice. The teams were gathered, discussing strategies and plays.

Just then, Gaurav's phone rang.

He glanced at the screen—Yogita.

"Hello," Gaurav said, wiping sweat off his forehead.

"Hi, still playing?" Yogita asked.

"No. Just resting on the ground."

"Come to the main gate."

"What?"

"Yes. Main gate."

Gaurav, slightly confused, walked towards the gate while still on the call. And then he saw her.

He slid his phone into his pocket. "What are you doing here?" he asked.

"You told me to come play cricket, remember?" Yogita said, wiping sweat off her forehead.

"I was joking, *yaar*."

"I know... but I couldn't focus in the office. Honestly, I don't even know what I'm doing with my life right now. So, I thought, why not come see you?"

Gaurav sighed and handed her his water bottle. "Oho. You're crazy, you know that?"

Yogita took a sip, looking around. "There are so many people here. Four or five teams, at least! And even girls are playing."

"Hmm. People come here for coaching. Some play tournaments too," Gaurav explained.

She glanced at the field, still processing the chaos of bats swinging, balls being chased, and the constant chatter of players.

"Come on," Gaurav said, motioning towards a shaded area. "Let's sit under the tin shed."

They walked over and sat down.

"Finished your office work?" Gaurav asked.

"No, man. Not yet. So much is still pending," Yogita replied.

"So, going to the office tomorrow?"

"No, I will go on Monday."

"Then Kundan will give you a proper scolding on Monday."

"I don't know what will happen on Monday. But I'm starting to get your point. I will treat my job just like a job. Won't let it take over me. What's the point of earning if it comes at the cost of your health? If it robs you of your mental peace?"

"And if he says he's firing you? Then what?"

"Then I'll leave. I'll search for another company. There has to be some place that doesn't suck the life out of people."

"Hmm. You've started caring about yourself. Good to hear. But you ruined my cricket practice today. Maybe you don't know, but I've kept my Saturdays reserved just for myself. From now on, Saturdays will be mine. Just me, doing what makes me happiest."

"Then I made a mistake by coming here. Disturbed you. Sorry for that. But I wanted to meet you. I feel good when I meet you."

"Control your emotions. You're giving me some signals here," Gaurav said with a smirk.

"Emotions don't listen to anyone. They stay where they feel good. And no, I don't have feelings for you," Yogita said, grinning slightly.

"Good. Because I'm already married. I don't want to get into this mess."

"When did I say 'marry me'? I just..." She stopped mid-sentence.

"Why did you stop? Complete it."

"Nothing. I just want to talk to you... and keep meeting you."

"Few more days left for me in the office. After that, you'll be somewhere, I'll be somewhere. Who knows when we'll meet again."

For a while, Yogita was silent.

Seeing her quiet, Gaurav spoke, "What happened? Why did you go silent?"

Yogita turned her face away and softly said, "Nothing." But her voice came from deep within her throat.

When she turned back, Gaurav saw tears rolling down her cheeks.

"Why are you crying? You're way too sensitive. I'm just a colleague. One comes, one goes, that's how it works. Don't get so emotional."

"For you, I might just be a colleague. But for me, you..." She trailed off again.

This time, Gaurav didn't ask her to complete the sentence. He didn't want to face that truth either.

Silence hung in the air.

Gaurav never thought Yogita would love him this much.

Yogita leaned in slightly and rested her head on his shoulder.

For a few moments, Gaurav stayed still, but then he spoke, "People are watching. My neighbor is here too. He'll go home and spread gossip everywhere. He doesn't know your name, but he'll make up some story."

"Handle it however you want. I don't care. I just want to be with you."

Ah, love. That relentless storm. Once it strikes, it drowns everything in its path.

From a distance, a voice called out, "Gaurav *bhai*, come fast! It's your turn to bat!"

"Let someone else play in my place. I'll come in a while," Gaurav shouted back.

"Go play," Yogita said, lifting her head off his shoulder.

"I'll drop you at Noida first. No practice today. You came all the way here just to see me, I can't just leave you alone. Come, I've got the car. Let me drop you off."

Both stood up, dusted off their jeans, and walked toward the car.

As they drove towards Noida, Yogita had already drowned her sorrows in endless conversation. She kept talking to Gaurav non-stop, filling the journey with everything under the sun—memories, random thoughts, work gossip, life philosophies.

Gaurav listened calmly, responding just enough to keep the conversation going, but careful never to fuel any expectations. He knew she was deeply lost in love.

The car slowed down near her apartment. Gaurav pulled over and parked on the side.

"We've reached," he said, shifting the gear to neutral.

"I didn't even realize how the journey flew by while talking to you," Yogita smiled.

"Hmm. Happens."

"Come upstairs. I'll make tea for you myself." There was a soft insistence in her voice.

"No, no. Your roommate must be there too. Won't feel right." He had no intention of going in and was trying to find a way out.

"She's gone on a trip. No one's at the apartment."

Gaurav sighed, leaning back. "Still, *yaar*. Try to understand."

Yogita didn't listen. Instead, she quickly opened his car door, grabbed the keys, and grinned. "Come with me if you want your keys back."

Gaurav glanced at her, exhaling lightly. She wasn't giving up. He stepped out. "Alright, fine. But at least give me the keys so I can lock the car."

She locked the car remotely, then gestured for him to follow.

With no option left, he walked behind her, climbing the stairs to the first floor.

Yogita pulled out the keys from her purse, unlocked the door, and stepped inside. Without missing a beat, she grabbed Gaurav's hand and pulled him in.

Inside, everything was neatly placed. The apartment smelled faintly of jasmine, and the soft lighting gave it a warm, cozy feel.

"You can freshen up in the washroom if you want. I'll make tea," Yogita said and stepped into the small kitchen.

Gaurav was covered in dust from the ground. He walked into the washroom, washed his face, hands, and feet, and returned. He wiped himself with a towel and sat down on the mattress spread on the floor.

There was no chair, no table—not even a proper bed. Yogita and her roommate slept on the floor itself. They lived on rent and deliberately kept fewer belongings, knowing that shifting to another place would be easier this way. Wherever their jobs took them, they found a place nearby, rented it, and adapted.

Most people did the same. Jobs were unpredictable—one day you were in one city, the next you were somewhere else.

"Nice room," Gaurav remarked casually.

"Thanks." Yogita placed the cups of tea on the floor.

"I noticed there's no furniture or bed—do you and your roommate sleep on just this mattress?"

"Yes."

Gaurav took a sip of tea.

"You made a good tea," he said.

"Thanks. I cook well too," Yogita replied with a playful smile.

"Now don't say 'stay for lunch.'"

"Fine, I won't," she said, taking a sip herself.

A few minutes later, Gaurav finished his tea and set the cup down. "Thanks for the tea. I should leave now."

"Seriously?" she asked, her voice holding a hint of longing.

"Yep," Gaurav said with a soft smile and stood up.

Yogita got up too, and before he could move, she wrapped her arms around him tightly.

Gaurav within seconds, pulled back and stepped away. "Don't test my patience," he said with a calm firmness. "After all, I'm a man. If I stay any longer, we'll end up doing something I'll— regret."

Without another word, he walked toward the door.

Yogita stood frozen in her spot, watching him leave. Within moments, uneasiness crept in. *Had she done something wrong? What if Gaurav was upset? What if he stopped talking to her?*

A storm of uncertainty churned in her mind.

Meanwhile, Gaurav started his car, played some ghazals, and drove home.

His mind kept replaying the scene in Yogita's room.

He felt sorry for her. On one side, she was struggling with job stress; on the other, she had feelings for him. And he knew—he could only bring her pain.

Earlier, she was just troubled about work. Now, love has made things messier.

Poor Yogita.

CHAPTER FIVE

Escaping Spreadsheets, Booking Mountains

It was Monday, Gaurav reached the office, but it was already 10:15 AM - way past his usual time. He parked his car and headed straight to the tea stall outside for a tea and a cigarette. Earlier, he used to rush to work on his car, always trying to be punctual. But now? He didn't care anymore. That's why he drove leisurely today.

By the time he checked in, it was 10:35 AM.

Gaurav noticed Kundan and Yogita talking near the corner of the floor—but the tone wasn't friendly.

"Yogita," Kundan said sharply, loud enough for nearby ears to catch, "We call people on Saturdays only when there's urgent work. If you're not serious about your job, just say so. You can follow Gaurav's path—serve your notice period and leave. But this *man-maani* won't work here."

Yogita didn't reply. Her eyes dropped to the floor, shoulders tight. She knew exactly what this was about—she had skipped Saturday's office and went to see Gaurav on the playground. It wasn't just about a missed day now. It had become a display of power.

She kept quiet, taking it all in without protest. After a pause, she said softly, "I'll finish the work, sir... as soon as I can." And walked back to her seat without looking up.

There was silence in her steps. No one clapped back at Kundan, no heroic speeches. Just a quiet girl carrying humiliation like invisible baggage.

Kundan had been waiting for Gaurav since morning. The moment he spotted him walking toward his seat, he intercepted him in the hallway. "Gaurav, there's an urgent task. I called you, but you didn't pick up the call."

Gaurav had deliberately ignored Kundan's call when he was on the way.

"Yes, sir, I was driving, so I couldn't answer. Tell me, what's the task?" Gaurav replied casually.

"The project you submitted last week has 15 corrections. You can do them later. First, fix the two urgent corrections that came in last night," Kundan said.

"Mail me the details, sir. I'll check and let you know how much time it'll take," Gaurav said.

"I need them done today. I have to show them to the clients tonight," Kundan added.

That hit a nerve. The moment Gaurav heard that these tasks had to be **completed by tonight**, his frustration spiked. He wasn't in the mood to work under that kind of pressure anymore. He paused for a moment before replying, then said, "If those are that much urgent please assign someone else. I will do those things at my own pace. I can't assure you tonight. If those will be doable then I will surely do it, but if I need extra time, then Sorry, I can't do it."

Kundan said nothing. Maybe he didn't have to. The look in his eyes said it all—he knew Gaurav's countdown had already begun, and the farewell was only a formality now.

Gaurav went to his seat and opened his mail. He checked the two latest corrections first. Then he thought, "Let's take a proper look at the previous mail, too." He hadn't fully gone through the 15 older corrections yet.

One by one, he started reading through them. As he reached correction number 11, he zoomed in and compared it with today's correction—same task, different wording. Suspicious, he checked the second "urgent" correction from today and matched it with the previous mail. It was correction number 13, again worded differently but essentially the same.

His blood boiled.

"Kundan's game was clear now." Instead of giving all 15 corrections at once, he was breaking them up into pairs, sometimes even one at a time, stretching the workload over 10–12 days.

Gaurav clenched his jaw. *"How shameless can people be? How do they even sleep at night after pulling off such cheap tricks?"* He smirked to himself. Alright, Kundan, let me show you what 'tonight' looks like for your precious task.

He got up and walked over to Yogita's desk.

"Hey, Yogita," he greeted.

"Hey Yogita, how are you?" Gaurav asked casually, sliding his chair a little closer.

"I'm okay," she said with a half-smile. "But got an earful from Kundan this morning. You remember—I skipped office on Saturday to join you at the cricket ground? Apparently, that's now a crime."

She laughed, but there was a sting hiding beneath the humor.

"Forget him," Gaurav said, waving it off. "He just loves acting like the HR police."

"Actually..." he leaned in, lowering his voice a notch. "A few days ago, I heard you talking on the phone—something about your birthday? You never finished the story. So, what's the plan? Party or secret mission?"

The way he asked it—light, teasing—cut through the tension like fresh air.

"Hmm, I'm thinking of hosting it in my room. But since you're the most unpredictable person ever, I'm inviting you first," she teased.

"You remember three months ago when you guys planned that Uttarakhand trip, but I messed it up?" Gaurav asked.

"Of course, I remember! We had booked our tickets and everything. You made us cancel at the last minute. Don't remind me of that, man! You totally ruined the mood," Yogita complained.

"I'm reminding you for a reason. What if we celebrate your birthday in Uttarakhand this time?" Gaurav suggested.

"Sounds great, but will Sunny and Kapil get a leave?" she asked.

"We'll plan it for the weekend—Saturday and Sunday. And for Monday or Friday, we'll just take a sick leave," he said, shrugging.

"Alright, let's discuss it over lunch," she agreed.

Just then, Gaurav's phone rang. It was Ruby.

"Yeah, tell me," he answered.

"I need to talk to you," Ruby's voice was sharp.

Gaurav immediately sensed the tension in her tone. Without wasting a second, he decided to step away and take the call privately. He walked briskly toward the terrace.

"Okay, now tell me. What happened? Why do you sound so angry?" he asked.

"You've resigned, haven't you?" Ruby's voice was sharp.

Gaurav froze for a moment. He hadn't expected her to find out so soon. But now, there was no way out. He had to admit it.

"Yeah. I was going to tell you yesterday, but I forgot," he said.

"You forgot? It's been many days since you resigned. You've been forgetting for that long?"

Gaurav sighed. "I thought you'd worry, so I didn't tell you."

"Of course, I'd worry! You know the salary you give me is barely enough. And now you've quit your job too? Listen, I'm not scolding you, I'm just making you understand—money is important. Either join back or at least start giving interviews somewhere else."

"I know, I know. We'll talk when I get home."

And with that, he hung up.

Gaurav went back to his seat. Ruby's words had left a lingering tension in his mind. She was right—money mattered. He sighed, opened the job portal, updated his latest resume, and even bought a premium package. Now, all he had to do was wait for interview calls.

At lunchtime, he met Sunny, Kapil, and Yogita in the cafeteria. The conversation quickly turned casual.

"Gaurav, since when did you start agreeing to trips?" Kapil asked, raising an eyebrow.

"Yeah, because of him, so many trips got canceled before. Or we just went without him," Sunny chimed in.

"*Yaar*, back then, I took work too seriously. The job was crushing me, and family responsibilities added to the pressure. But now, I feel lighter. I don't care about office stress anymore," Gaurav said, leaning back in his chair.

"Obviously, why would you? You're in your notice period after all," Yogita smirked.

"So, coming Saturday, we're finally going to Mussoorie, right?" Gaurav asked.

Everyone nodded in agreement.

"How are we traveling—train, flight, or bus?" Kapil asked.

"Let's take my car. Just four of us, it'll be comfortable. I'll drive, and if I get tired, Kapil can take over," Gaurav suggested.

"You? Driving all the way?" Sunny raised a skeptical brow.

"Yeah, yeah, don't worry," Gaurav assured him.

"Will *Bhabhiji* let you go?" Yogita asked, referring to Ruby.

"I'll convince her. She usually says no, but I'll manage. And if she doesn't agree, I'll go anyway," Gaurav shrugged.

"Listen, only go if she says yes. I mean, convince her first. Her approval is important," Yogita insisted.

"Why are you taking *Bhabhi's* side?" Sunny asked, amused.

"You boys don't get it—women don't like it when decisions are made without them," Yogita shot back, throwing a sly look at Sunny.

"Yogita is right. You'll understand when you get married," Gaurav muttered. "Not something you can figure out right now."

"But will she really make a scene if you don't tell her? Does she actually fight with you? I just heard a rumor," Sunny said.

"She was fine earlier, man. But I don't know—she's become irritable. Always picking fights over the smallest things. I can't figure out whether she's changed or I have. But I kept silent at home. You know what? ***If women keep striking a man for his family, habits, finances, and explanations , he will choose silence as his shield to escape the fight.***"

"That's why I am telling you to inform her. Better do it today itself," Yogita reminded him.

"Yeah, yeah, I will," Gaurav nodded.

"Alright, let's get back to the office. I have to finish work before this Friday, or Kundan will eat me alive. And if I don't finish it, this trip might get canceled because of me. He'll make me work on Saturday!" Yogita said anxiously before heading back.

Sunny, Gaurav, and Kapil stayed back for a while, and then, as always, drifted towards Chotu's tea stall for a cigarette.

The evening was settling in.

Some people were leaving the office, some were packing their bags, while others were busy updating their leads on their work status.

Gaurav stood up from his seat. "Sir, those two points didn't get completed today. They'll be done by tomorrow."

Kundan frowned. "Those two tasks were urgent. I told you I needed them by this evening!"

"I already told you, If you need them urgently, you should assign them to someone else. I'm not stretching office hours," Gaurav said, slinging his bag over his shoulder. His tone was calm but firm—he wasn't going to budge.

Without waiting for a response, he walked towards the exit.

Kundan just stood there, staring after him, speechless. No one usually talked to him like that. But Gaurav? He was done playing by the rules.

Gaurav reached home, holding chocolates and flowers for his wife and daughter. He stepped inside, expecting a warm welcome—at least a smile. But Ruby barely glanced at the gifts. She had only one thing on her mind.

"Alright, now tell me. Why did you resign?" she asked, straight to the point.

"Can I at least wash my hands first? Drink some water? Sit down for a moment? You didn't even let me breathe before starting your interrogation," Gaurav sighed. He placed the chocolates and flowers on the table, set his laptop aside, and walked into the washroom.

Ruby went to the kitchen, filled a glass of water, and waited for him to settle down.

A few minutes later, Gaurav sat on the couch, took a long sip, and placed the glass on the table. He could feel Ruby's piercing gaze on him, her unspoken questions hanging in the air.

"Listen," Gaurav said, finally meeting her eyes. "I'll tell you why I resigned. I'll explain why I did what I did."

Ruby folded her arms.

"If you want to start something new, you must end something first," Gaurav said, leaning forward. "And remember this—whatever you start now, one day, you'll have to end it too. It's the cycle of life. If you keep ending and starting things by choice, you'll always feel alive, excited, full of energy. But if you don't, if you let things end on their own without taking charge, one day they'll collapse in front of you, and that day you'll feel helpless, stuck, and miserable."

Ruby frowned slightly, still processing. Gaurav knew she wasn't convinced yet.

"Let me give you an example," he continued. "Lately, you've been complaining about how boring your mornings have become. If you start going for a morning walk, that means you'll have to end something—your morning laziness, your habit of waking up late. That's how change happens."

Ruby didn't say anything.

"If I want a new job with better opportunities, I have to end the current one first," Gaurav explained. "Anything new requires letting go of something old. Otherwise, if I just sit and wait, life will eventually force that change on me—but by then, I'd feel powerless. I resigned because I wanted to be the one in control, not the one at fate's mercy."

Silence.

For the first time in years, Ruby looked like she had nothing to say. No arguments, no counter-questions, no lectures.

But after a moment, she shook her head, took a deep breath, and said, "Fine. All this philosophy is great. But start looking for a new job quickly. Money is more important than all this wisdom."

A smirk formed on Gaurav's lips. He knew she was right. But he also knew—this conversation wasn't just about money. It was about life, change, and taking control before it was too late.

The mood at home was neutral—until Gaurav brought up the trip.

"Listen, my office colleagues and I are planning a trip to Mussoorie this Saturday. I mean, the plan is set, but I wanted to talk to you about it first," Gaurav said cautiously.

Ruby's expression changed instantly, her face hardening. "So, you have money for a trip, but not for the things we actually need?" she snapped.

Gaurav sighed. He had expected some resistance, but not this level of frustration. "*Yaar*, it's not like that. I just thought..."

"You thought what, exactly?" Ruby cut him off, her tone sharper now. "You barely take your job seriously, and now you're planning vacations with your office friends? Have you even thought about where things are heading with your career?"

"This trip has been planned for weeks," Gaurav said, trying to keep his cool.

"And in all these weeks, did you once think about how we are managing things at home?" Ruby shot back. "Bills keep piling up, and you act like everything is fine. Meanwhile, you're off to Mussoorie like some carefree bachelor?"

"Ruby, come on..."

"No, Gaurav. This isn't just about this trip. It's about the way you keep ignoring reality. You want to run off with your office friends for a weekend and then what? Come back and pretend like there's no tension at home?"

Gaurav exhaled, rubbing his forehead. This conversation was spiraling far beyond what he had imagined.

"Just cancel the trip," Ruby said finally, crossing her arms.

Gaurav clenched his jaw, frustration boiling inside him. "I'm not canceling anything, Ruby," he said, his voice sharper now. "I've already committed to this trip, and I will go."

Ruby's eyes widened in fury. "Oh, so now it's just your decision, huh? You don't care about this family, about our struggles? You just care about running off with your office buddies?"

"That's not true!" Gaurav shot back. "I bust my ass every day at work too! I deserve a break! Just because things are tough doesn't mean I have to put my life on hold forever."

Ruby scoffed. "A break? You're irresponsible, Gaurav! This isn't college anymore where you can just do whatever you feel like."

"Don't start that again," he said, exhaustion creeping into his voice. "This trip—it's just a few days. Why do you have to make it such a big deal?"

"Because it is a big deal!" Ruby yelled. "I deal with everything alone while you pretend nothing is wrong! You never think ahead, and we always end up struggling because of it!"

Their voices kept rising, words crashing like thunder in the small space.

And then—Khushi's wail cut through the chaos. Both of them froze. Their daughter stood in the doorway, her tiny face scrunched up in fear and confusion.

Ruby immediately stepped toward her. "Khushi—"

Silence hung in the air. The fight was over. At least for now.

CHAPTER SIX

WHEN PEACE FADED IN THE HILLS

In the excitement of going on the trip, no one realized how quickly the past 3–4 days flew by. It was Saturday today, and everyone was buzzing with excitement.

As planned from day one, Kapil, Sunny, Yogita, and Gaurav finally gathered at 7 AM, all pumped up to leave for Mussoorie. Each of them had been suffocating under corporate pressure, and this trip felt like a much-needed escape—a few days of freedom from the cage they had been stuck in.

"Kapil, put the route on Google Maps," Gaurav said.

Kapil tapped his screen, set the map, and fixed the phone onto the mobile holder.

"It shows seven hours," Kapil muttered.

"No worries. Gaurav, drive at your own pace. We're in no rush," Yogita assured him.

Sunny connected his phone to the car's Bluetooth, and music started playing. The mood was set. Yogita unzipped her bag and pulled out packets of Lay's, wafers, and cold drinks, handing them over to everyone.

The car echoed with laughter, friendly banter, and random leg-pulling.

Yogita noticed that Gaurav had been unusually quiet for a while.

"Gaurav, why are you so silent?" she asked, nudging him.

"Nothing," he replied, shaking his head.

"Let me guess," Yogita smirked. "Did *bhabhi* scold you this morning? Something like—'You're going on a trip alone? Take me along too!'"

As soon as she said it, the entire group burst into laughter.

Gaurav sighed. "*Yaar*, we had a huge fight last night. She was completely against the trip. But I told her straight—I'm going, no matter what."

"Oho, so *bhabhi* didn't want you to go, and you just stubbornly left?" Sunny teased.

"Yeah. I don't know why she seems out of her mind most of the time, man. Gets angry over everything and starts arguing."

"Don't say that, *yaar*," Yogita said, shaking her head. "We're on a trip, Right now, forget all that sulking, And listen, save the fights for when you get home. "

The group erupted into laughter again, the tension dissolving into carefree conversation.

After driving for about three hours, they decided to take a break at a roadside *dhaba* for some tea. Stretching their legs, sipping their tea, they let the journey sink in before hitting the road again.

Around 7 PM, they finally reached Mussoorie's '**Welcome Hotel**' where they had booked rooms in advance from Noida. The excitement that had kept them charged throughout the day had started to wear off. Fatigue crept in.

Once inside the hotel, they ordered tea again—because what's a trip without endless cups of tea? Some sprawled on the bed, stretching lazily, while others slumped onto the sofa, legs stretched out, unwilling to move even an inch.

Kapil, exhausted, tried to lie back, but Gaurav mischievously pulled the pillow from under his head.

"Bro, have some mercy," Kapil groaned.

"Mercy is for the weak," Gaurav smirked, sinking deeper into his couch.

"What's the plan for the evening?" Sunny asked, stretching his arms.

"Arrange some bottles of rum. And chicken," Gaurav declared.

"Let's go for mutton today. It's cold here in Mussoorie. Mutton would be perfect," Kapil suggested.

"Fine by me," Gaurav nodded. Then, turning to Yogita, he asked, "And you? What do you want to eat and drink?"

"I'll have a beer. But please, no one tells anyone at the office," she smirked.

The room erupted into laughter.

"Alright then, freshen up, everyone. It's already seven. Let's kick off the party by eight," Kapil announced.

"Chill, man. What's the rush? The night's ours," Gaurav said, sinking further into the couch as if he had no intention of moving anytime soon.

Yogita stretched and got up. "I'll stay in a separate room. This one, or the one next door? You guys decide."

"Take the one next door. These guys won't move for another couple of hours. You can freshen up, settle your stuff, and claim it as yours," Kapil laughed.

Yogita picked up her bag and walked toward the adjacent room.

By 8 PM, the evening had set in. The balcony was surprisingly spacious—almost big enough to carve out an extra room. Nothing like the cramped, tiny balconies back in Delhi NCR. But then again, this was a tourist hotel, designed to offer comfort, breathing space, and a view worth remembering.

The food and drinks were set up neatly on the balcony. Yogita had taken charge and arranged everything perfectly. Everyone settled down, sitting cross-legged on the floor, soaking in the crisp Mussoorie air.

Gaurav was the first to crack open a can of beer and handed it to Yogita. Then, he uncapped the bottle of rum and started pouring drinks into glasses, carefully measuring out pegs. The clinking of glasses signaled the beginning of the night.

With the first sip down, the mood shifted. Conversations turned lively, laughter echoed in the air. Gossip started flowing—one story juicier than the last.

Mutton, momos, namkeens, peanuts, salad, corn—everything was being used as sides to go with rum and beer, each bite making the drinks smoother, each sip making the food taste better.

After downing two pegs each, the group was almost completely immersed in the buzz of the night. Conversations flowed effortlessly, voices grew louder, laughter became unrestrained. Even Yogita had finished her first beer and casually cracked open another beer can, as if she had done this a hundred times before.

"Didn't you say just one?" Gaurav teased, raising an eyebrow.

Yogita smirked, taking a sip. "One can at a time."

The night had only just begun, and it was already turning into one to remember.

Yogita took a sip of her beer and sighed, "Kundan has been stressing me out like crazy." Saying this, she picked up a piece of mutton and started chewing, as if the food could absorb some of her frustration.

"Why are you even worrying so much? I'm here, na," Sunny winked and, without warning, dropped his head onto Yogita's lap.

"You're too drunk now. Sit properly," Yogita protested, using all her strength to push Sunny upright.

"Mujhe to ghanta farak nahi padta kundan se." ("I couldn't care less about Kundan anymore,") Gaurav said, taking another sip, letting the warmth of the drink settle in. Then, a smirk tugged at his lips.

He paused for dramatic effect, glancing at everyone, waiting for their curiosity to build. Then, with a smirk, he finally spoke,

"When I was a kid, I loved wearing my father's shoes. They weren't fancy, and they were way too big for me. But somehow, I loved them. My tiny feet barely filled them, and every step felt clumsy, but I still walked in them anyway. My father would walk beside me, smiling as he watched me. I'd fall—again and again—but I never stopped wearing them. Every morning, I'd slip them on, like they were mine.

Years later, when I moved to Delhi from Ayodhya for a job, I had nothing. No money, no work. Then, when I finally landed my first job, I had to join a new company, which meant dressing formally. But there was a problem—I didn't own formal black shoes. So I borrowed a pair from a friend. They were two sizes bigger than mine. I tightened the laces as much as I could, wore thick socks to make them fit, and hoped for the best.

For days, I walked into the office wearing those shoes. But I slipped, stumbled—fell more than once. I never wore them with happiness. One day, frustrated, I took them off and tossed them away.

And this resignation? Think of it the same way. Just like I threw away those ill-fitting shoes, I've thrown away a job that never fit me."

"So, are you saying I should quit too?" Yogita asked, watching him closely.

Gaurav leaned back and smirked. "First, tell me this—why was I happy wearing my father's oversized shoes?"

Everyone exchanged glances but stayed silent.

"Because I wasn't afraid of falling. My father was there to catch me. And when I did fall, he would pick me up, rub my knee gently, and tell me to keep walking.

Now, I've quit this job, and I'm searching for new shoes—ones that fit me perfectly, ones that don't make me stumble. Because now, if I fall, no one will catch me.

Whether you quit or not, that's your decision. You have to find your own path. I'm looking for a fresh start—I don't know where it'll lead, but I've emptied myself for now. No shoes, No burdens, nothing weighing me down."

Gaurav swirled his drink slowly, his eyes distant. The conversation had taken a turn—from casual banter to something raw, something real.

The clock had struck eleven. Conversations flowed freely as the drinks did, and the weariness of the day mingled with the intoxication—forming a perfect recipe for sleep.

Kapil had already surrendered, crashing onto the bed without a second thought. But Sunny had a different plan. He had been waiting for this moment for over a year.

"Yogita, your presence made this trip even better," Sunny said.

"Hmm, all thanks to Gaurav. He planned it. That's why I like him," Yogita replied.

"What? Do you love him?" Sunny asked, surprised.

"No, just as a friend. He's really nice," Yogita laughed.

"And what about me? Am I not good?" Sunny joked.

"No. You seem crazy to me. Always confused."

Gaurav burst out laughing. "Hear that? Your insult! You asked for it!"

Sunny's face fell.

"I'm going to sleep now. It's too late," Yogita said.

"Sit for a little longer. The night's still young," Sunny insisted.

"No, *yaar*. It's too late."

With that, Yogita left for her room.

Sunny nodded, took a deep breath, and followed her.

Inside the room, Yogita frowned at him. "Why are you here?"

"I want to tell you something."

"Yes, tell me."

"I love you."

"Look Sunny, we both are friends. And let this friendship remain limited to friendship only."

"Please accept my proposal."

"There is no compulsion in love. I have already given my answer."

Sunny pushed Yogita towards a wall and stuck both her hands to the wall.

"You did not understand what I wanted,"Sunny tried to kiss Yogita on the lips.

Yogita tried to break free from him forcefully and, after freeing herself, ran towards the bed.

Sunny also ran in the same direction and then caught Yogita by the waist.

Yogita started screaming, "Save me, save me..."

Gaurav was sitting on the balcony and listening to ghazals on his phone. He heard some vague voice. He immediately paused a ghazal, then when he listened carefully, it was Yogita's voice.

He ran and reached Yogita's room.

He saw that Sunny was sitting on top of Yogita and he was trying to control her by using force.

Gaurav grabbed Sunny's collar and pulled him and punched him 4-5 times on his face. Sunny fell on the ground with so much force, Gaurav then kicked him. Sunny almost fainted. He was so intoxicated that he couldn't even stand up. Gaurav grabbed him by the leg and dragged him and took him to another room where Kapil was sleeping.

He came back to Yogita's room.

Yogita was sitting on the bed and crying. There were tears in her eyes.

Gaurav stepped closer, his voice gentle as he patted her head. "Please don't cry. This is all my fault. I planned this trip... and because of that, everything happened."

Yogita didn't say anything, just kept crying.

Gaurav stood near her for a few minutes.

After some time, Yogita said, "Are all boys like this? They just want to satisfy their lust with the girl."

Gaurav sat near her and said, "Yes you are right, some people are like that."

Both of them remained silent for some time, Gaurav kept caressing Yogita's head on his shoulder.

"Gaurav, thank you, you saved me. I like you from the bottom of my heart. Don't ever break my heart."

"Never."

They sat there, side by side, saying little but sharing everything in the silences between their words. Gaurav kept talking softly—stories, distractions, anything to keep her mind from spiraling. He could see it in her eyes—the mix of pain, relief, and the effect of far too much beer.

Yogita had clearly drunk more than she could handle. Her eyelids grew heavier with each passing minute, her head slowly resting against his shoulder. Gaurav himself wasn't exactly sober, but he held his ground, letting the alcohol soften the edges of his thoughts without blurring his intent.

Nearly an hour passed like that, wrapped in warmth and quiet. Eventually, the alcohol took over completely, and Yogita drifted off.

"Just sleep," he whispered gently, brushing her hair back as she settled in. No questions. No moves. No complications.

Gaurav slowly made her sleep on the bed and put a blanket over her. He kept watching him sleeping for some time and was regretting the incident which had happened some time ago by Sunny.

Exhaustion weighed heavily on him. The long drive had already drained him, and now the alcohol was pulling him further into a haze of drowsiness. His body felt sluggish, his thoughts slow.

Without much thought, he reached for a nearby blanket, spread it over himself, and lay down on the mat on the floor.

CHAPTER SEVEN

NO PAUSE BETWEEN PROBLEMS

The morning after a night of heavy drinking always feels different—an unbearable headache, a nauseous feeling, and a strange warmth radiating inside the body. Kapil felt exactly that when he woke up at 8 AM.

He looked around, confused. The room was empty. His heart skipped a beat. He sat up abruptly and scanned the surroundings before stepping outside. He walked toward the adjacent room, noticing the door was slightly ajar. Pushing it open gently, he saw Gaurav sprawled on the floor and Yogita asleep on the bed.

Relieved, he quietly shut the door and returned to his own room. At least these two were here. But Sunny—where was he? Kapil picked up his phone, intending to call him. Just then, he noticed a message from Sunny.

"Kapil, I wasn't feeling well, so I left for Noida early. Don't worry, just thought I'd inform you."

Kapil frowned. Why would Sunny leave for Noida all of a sudden—especially today, on Yogita's birthday?

Without wasting time, he walked back to Gaurav and Yogita's room and knocked loudly, pretending to be hotel staff. "Room service! Room service!" he called out.

The knock startled both of them awake. Gaurav groggily got up and opened the door.

"Oh, it's you! I thought it was an actual hotel staff," Gaurav muttered, walking back to his chair and slumping into it.

"That's exactly why I did it—so you'd wake up thinking it's someone important," Kapil smirked and took a sip from the water bottle he had picked up. Gaurav stretched his hand out, and Kapil handed him the bottle without saying anything.

"Sunny went home," Kapil said, breaking the silence.

"What? When?" Gaurav asked, his voice sharper now.

"This morning. I got a message from him."

"He had to leave. What face would he have left to talk to me now?" Yogita said, her tone distant.

Kapil frowned. "What do you mean?"

Neither Gaurav nor Yogita responded.

"Come on, tell me!" Kapil pressed, growing impatient.

"I'll tell you later. First, go get some tea from the shop outside," Gaurav said.

"Cigarette?" Kapil asked.

"Yeah, let's go outside. We'll smoke there," Gaurav replied.

The two stepped out of the hotel and walked about fifty meters to a small roadside stall. The hotel had rooms for lodging but no kitchen, so everything had to be brought from outside. The air smelled of fresh tea, morning dew, and last night's conversations left unfinished.

As Gaurav took a drag from his cigarette, he recounted the entire incident from last night.

Kapil listened, stunned. His mind raced as he tried to process everything.

"Bro, what must Yogita be thinking about all of us now?" Kapil muttered.

"What can we even do about a guy like that?" Gaurav exhaled a puff of smoke, shaking his head.

Kapil sighed. "I don't know, man. I feel ashamed to even face Yogita now. This was messed up."

"Hm."

"So... did you really beat Sunny up badly?"

"Nah, just three or four solid punches. He dropped to the floor pretty quick. Then I dragged him into the other room and left him there."

"You did the right thing. I had no idea he'd stoop this low," Kapil said, picking up the steaming kettle of tea the shopkeeper had just handed over.

They exchanged a glance and wordlessly gestured toward the hotel.

As they walked back, the silence between them wasn't just about exhaustion—it carried the weight of everything that had happened.

By the time Gaurav and Kapil entered the room with tea, Yogita had already freshened up. Everyone settled down with their cups, letting the warmth seep in. The plan was simple—stay in the room till evening, rest, recharge, and then head out for a stroll before the big cake-cutting moment at night.

The day passed in lazy conversations and stolen naps. No rush, no deadlines—just the comfort of doing nothing. By evening, the group finally stepped out, eager to explore a bit of Mussoorie's charm. They wandered through the serene paths near Waterfall, where the sound of cascading water mixed with the distant chatter of tourists. The air was crisp, carrying the scent of pine and damp earth. A few selfies, some laughter, and a quiet moment by the water—it was the kind of evening that felt effortlessly perfect.

By 8 PM, they were back in the room, the excitement building up. The cake sat on the table, waiting. Gaurav dimmed the lights, and the candles flickered to life. It wasn't just about cutting a cake—it was about marking a moment, sealing a memory. And as the first slice was made, the room filled with cheers, laughter, and the sweet taste of celebration. Yogita fed cake to Gaurav and Kapil one by one.

Coke, cake, namkeens—everything was on the table, the mood light and celebratory. In the middle of it all, Gaurav pulled out a small box and handed it to Yogita.

"A gift for you," he said, smiling.

Yogita opened it and gasped. A wristwatch—simple, elegant, perfect. Tears welled up in her eyes as she looked at him, overwhelmed. She hugged him tightly. "Thank you, Gaurav. This means so much."

And just then—his phone rang.

The sudden shrill tone sliced through the warm, comforting atmosphere. He glanced at the screen. Sidhu *Bhai*.

"Hello, Gaurav ji," Sidhu's voice came through, slightly hurried.

"Yes, Sidhu *Bhai*? What happened?" Gaurav asked casually, still lost in the glow of the moment.

"You need to come to the hospital. Immediately."

Something in Sidhu's tone made Gaurav sit upright. "Hospital?" His pulse quickened.

"Yes," Sidhu continued, voice growing heavier. "Your wife is serious."

Gaurav felt a chill run down his spine. His hands turned cold. "What?"

Sidhu took a deep breath. "She's admitted. Khanna ji and I brought her here just now."

Gaurav shot up from his seat. The room, the people, the cake—everything blurred around him. "What happened to her?" His voice was barely steady now.

There was silence for half a second. And then Sidhu spoke,"You need to come. Now. Your wife tried to kill herself. She had taken poison."

"What? Poison?" he repeated, as if saying it aloud would somehow make it less real.

His voice barely came out—a whisper, a breathless plea for clarity.

"Yes, Gaurav ji," Sidhu's voice was urgent, pressing. "She's admitted. The doctors... they're trying to remove the poison from her body."

The word hit him like a blow to the chest. His mind raced, searching for explanations. He was thinking... How? When? Why?

Sidhu's voice was heavy. "There's a note. I'm sorry, Gaurav Ji, but I read it."

Gaurav felt a sharp jolt in his chest. "A note? What kind of note? What does it say?"

Sidhu hesitated for a moment, then spoke, his tone grave. "It says—'*I know you went to Mussoorie because of Yogita. You two love each other. I also know you both spent the night in the same room. I can't tolerate this. Stay with her. Bye.*'"

Gaurav's head spun. His thoughts crashed into each other, a storm raging inside him. This couldn't be happening. How did she even—why did she?

He shut his eyes tight, forcing himself to think straight. "Sidhu *bhai*, stay at the hospital. Please. I'm leaving right now—I'll be there by morning. Till then, I'll send my brother-in-law over."

The room had gone eerily silent. The laughter, the celebration, the warmth—it had all vanished.

Yogita and Kapil stared at Gaurav, sensing the shift in the air, the tension gripping his face.

Yogita finally broke the silence. "What happened?"

Gaurav swallowed hard. Slowly, he looked at her, and then, with measured words, he told them everything.

"Kapil, start packing. We have to leave now," Yogita said, urgency in her voice.

Gaurav was still trying to make sense of everything. "I don't understand. How did all this reach my wife?"

"No idea," Yogita replied, her face clouded with confusion.

Gaurav's patience snapped. His fists clenched as he turned to Kapil. "Did you talk to my wife? Did you make this mess?"

Kapil's eyes widened. "No, Gaurav *bhai*. But if anyone could pull this off, it's Sunny."

Gaurav narrowed his eyes. "Call him. Put him on speaker. I want to hear what he has to say."

Kapil dialed Sunny, his hands slightly shaking. The phone rang, and then—

"Hello, Kapil," Sunny's voice came through.

"You reached Noida?" Kapil asked, masking his intentions.

"Yeah. Why? What's up?"

Kapil took a calculated risk. "I had a fallout with Gaurav today too. We need to do something."

Sunny chuckled. "Oh, I already got my revenge, bro."

Kapil exchanged a quick glance with Gaurav. "Really? How?"

"I called his wife. Told her everything about him and Yogita."

Kapil kept his tone steady. "How did you even get her number?"

Sunny laughed like it was all a game. "Getting numbers isn't hard. She follows me on social media. I sent her a message, got her number, and told her the whole story. Stirred the fire between them. Now, let's see how this plays out."

"She's in the hospital, brother... fighting between life and death," said Kapil.

"What? How did all this happen?" Sunny asked, shocked.

"Your words planted deep doubts in her mind... that's why she consumed poison."

"Oh my god."

"I'll talk later. We're coming back now."

The call ended, but the silence in the room was suffocating.

Gaurav's fingers curled into fists. His pulse pounded in his ears. **Sunny had destroyed everything**. I will kill him.

The celebration was over. The night had flipped into a nightmare.

"This trip is going to be unforgettable," Gaurav muttered, shaking his head.

"Hmm... one problem after another," Yogita sighed.

Kapil leaned forward, curiosity written all over his face. "Okay, tell me the truth—do you both actually love each other?"

Gaurav exhaled sharply. "Bro, there's nothing like that. We're just good friends, that's all."

Yogita nodded, backing him up. "Yeah, exactly. There's nothing more."

Gaurav ran a hand through his hair, frustration creeping into his voice. "And yeah, it was my mistake that I ended up in Yogita's room that night. I didn't even realize it—I was too drunk and slept on the floor." He paused, glancing at Yogita. "I wasn't thinking straight."

Yogita gave a small, reassuring smile. "It's okay, Gaurav. Let's not overthink it."

But the air between them still felt heavy—like an unfinished story, hanging between explanation and emotion.

CHAPTER EIGHT

GUILT IN THE EYES

It was 6 AM when Gaurav finally pulled over, his hands stiff on the steering wheel. After driving all night, he had safely dropped everyone back to Noida.

"Bye, Yogita. See you at the office tomorrow—though I'm definitely taking a leave today," he said, his voice laced with exhaustion.

"I think I'll come with you to the hospital," Yogita said, her voice gentle.

"No, no... please," Gaurav replied quickly, waving his hand. "If she sees you, things might just get worse. She's already angry. One look at you and she'll erupt again."

Yogita frowned, a little hurt but understanding.

"Trust me," Gaurav added, lowering his voice. "You guys go ahead. I'll handle this mess."

There was silence for a second—one of those awkward, honest silences you can only have with someone who knows too much.

"Bye, take care. Call me if you need anything," Yogita replied.

"Bye, Gaurav," Kapil added.

"Bye."

With that, Gaurav watched them walk away, then started his drive toward Delhi. His eyes burned from the lack of sleep, but his mind had only one focus—getting to the hospital. He punched in the location on the map and accelerated down the road.

An hour later, he reached. The hospital loomed ahead, sterile and quiet in the early morning haze.

Sidhu and Khanna uncle greeted him with a brief nod, but his attention was on Gajendra, his brother-in-law.

"How is Ruby now?" Gaurav asked, his voice tight.

"She's stable. You can go see her," Gajendra responded.

Gajendra knew about the note Ruby had left behind but never once doubted Gaurav's loyalty. Still, there was something in his stance, in the way he stood there, like he was waiting for an explanation.

Sidhu and Khanna ji also wanted answers, but they could see the exhaustion in Gaurav's eyes, the way his body slumped slightly. He had just returned from Mussoorie, sleep-deprived, and clearly drained. No one pressed him for details—not yet.

"Come with me," Gajendra said.

Gajendra walked him to Ruby's ward. The room was dimly lit, silent except for the soft hum of machines.

She was asleep.

Gaurav stepped closer, hesitated for a moment, then softly spoke. "Ruby."

Her eyelids fluttered open. For a long second, they just stared at each other. No words, just the weight of everything unsaid hanging between them.

Then—she turned her gaze away.

Gaurav swallowed hard, moved to her bedside, and sat down. Slowly, hesitantly, he reached out and took her hand.

"What was the need to take such a drastic step? You could've just talked to me," Gaurav said, his voice steady, calm—but firm."

"I know everything. Sunny told me everything. There's no need for explanations," Ruby replied, her tone carrying both hurt and finality.

"Okay. And tomorrow, if Kapil calls you from my office and says I have an affair with Shivani too, would you believe him? You know Shivani, right? My badminton partner?"

Ruby didn't respond.

"Answer me, Ruby."

No answer.

"Fine, imagine if both Yogita and Shivani had come on this trip. Today, Sunny called you. Tomorrow, Kapil could have called and said I'm with Shivani too. Would you believe him?"

Ruby was silent again.

"I am already struggling with this situation—why would I deliberately complicate my life even more by having such an affair?" Gaurav said, exhaling lightly. There was no frustration in his voice now, just clarity.

Ruby finally broke her silence and said, "Why did Yogita come to see you at the cricket ground? You even dropped her off at her flat in Noida. I know everything. Sidhu's wife told me a few days ago. But now, after what Sunny said, it's clear—you and Yogita are having an affair. Go to her. Why would you need me anymore?"

He replied, "She's just a coworker, nothing more. She was under a lot of work pressure, so she came to watch the cricket match just to ease her mind. Please don't let all this create doubt. *Gajendra Bhaiya, aap hi samjhao isko.*(Gajendra *Bhaiya*, please talk to her.)"

Gajendra spoke, breaking the uneasy silence. "Sister, Gaurav is right. You can't just believe what others say over his word. There needs to be trust between the two of you. I know Gaurav very well—he's not that kind of person. I have complete faith in him. If there had been something like that going on, I would've spoken to him myself before you ever had to. But there's nothing like that."

Ruby looked away, her voice trembling. "How am I supposed to believe there's nothing going on? I still can't wrap my head around it."

The tension in the room was thick, like the silence before a storm. Things were spiraling. Ruby had drawn her battle lines, standing firm in her doubt.

Just then, the door creaked open. Sidhu stepped into the hospital ward, with Sunny trailing behind him, a nervous wreck.

Before Gaurav could say anything, Sunny folded his hands. "Gaurav *bhai*... please forgive me. I had no idea bhabhi ji would take such a drastic step after hearing my words. I thought she'd fight with you, maybe give you some tension... I swear, I never meant for it to go this far. Never imagined it would end with her in a hospital bed."

He slowly turned toward Ruby, guilt etched across his face. "*Bhabhi ji,* I had a fight with Gaurav in Mussoorie. I got angry and... I said terrible things to you just to get back at him. But the truth is, everyone at the office knows Gaurav. He might be a bit impulsive at times, but he doesn't have anything going on with Yogita—or anyone else."

"So it was you who said all that over the phone," Gajendra said, narrowing his eyes at Sunny.

Sunny nodded miserably. "Yes, *bhaiya*. It was me. But the moment I heard bhabhi ji was in the hospital, I wasn't able to breathe properly. I know I messed up. But I'm not so heartless that I'd risk someone's life for petty revenge. You won't believe it—I haven't slept since yesterday. All night, I kept praying to God—please, just let her be okay. I promised myself, first thing in the morning, I'd come and apologize."

He looked at Gaurav with moist eyes. "Gaurav *bhai*, do whatever you feel is right. Yell at me, slap me, cut all ties if you want. I deserve it. I'm right here."

There was a pause. A strange, hollow silence.

No one said a word.

Then Gajendra's voice cut through. Calm, but clear. "Ruby, now you've heard it all. Don't let what outsiders say ruin what you two have. Relationships aren't made of just love. They're made of trust."

Ruby's eyes welled up. She turned to Gaurav, her voice cracking, barely above a whisper. "I'm... I'm so sorry, Gaurav. I didn't know my habit of doubting would grow so toxic... I never thought it would reach this point."

Tears slid down her cheeks, she said, "I should have trusted you. I should have known better. I don't deserve your forgiveness, but... I really hope you can find a little space in your heart to forgive me."

"It's ok, But I just don't understand—how could you not think about our daughter, Khushi, before taking such a terrible step? Please don't ever do something this reckless again. Where is Khushi?" Gaurav said.

"She's with my wife," Gajendra replied.

"Thank you *Bhaiya*." Gaurav said and looked at Ruby, "You rest Ruby. I'll go speak to the doctors about your discharge. Khushi must be crying without us." Gaurav said, standing up and leaving the room.

Gaurav met the doctor, keeping his tone collected. "How soon can Ruby be discharged?"

"She's stable now. We'll keep her under observation for a few more hours. If everything remains fine, she can go home today," the doctor replied.

"Alright," Gaurav said, nodding.

It was 10 a.m. Gaurav pulled out his phone and sent a message to Kundan at work:

"I'm on sick leave today."

No Explanation, no excuses , no sorry, no please.

"Sunny, you have to go to the office, right?" Gaurav said, his tone calm but carrying something unspoken beneath it.

"Yes," Sunny replied, eyes flickering with guilt.

"Then go. I'll talk to you... at the office."

That line—simple, but heavy—hung in the air like a courtroom verdict. Sunny felt his stomach drop. The way Gaurav said it, not with anger, not with bitterness, but with a quiet firmness—that scared him more.

He wanted to explain, to defend himself again, but Gaurav looked exhausted, not just in body but in spirit. Standing there in that hospital ward, juggling pain, responsibility, and a shattered relationship, Gaurav didn't have the energy for confrontation.

So Sunny nodded. Without another word, he turned around and walked out, each step feeling like it echoed across a courtroom floor. Whatever conversation was coming in the office... he knew it wouldn't be easy.

Gaurav reached the reception area and met Sidhu and Mr. Khanna.

"I really want to thank you both," Gaurav said, his tone steady yet heartfelt. "You brought Ruby to the hospital just in time. I'll never forget that."

Khanna Uncle smiled. "That's what neighbors are for, Gaurav. We look out for each other."

Gaurav nodded, then turned to Sidhu, his expression tightening slightly. "But Sidhu *bhai*, I'll be honest—I'm a little upset with you. You added fuel to the fire. You know my wife tends to be suspicious. Why did you even mention that stuff to your wife? You also know how women can... share things with each other."

Sidhu glanced at the floor, guilt creeping up his face like a shadow. "I said it to my wife casually... just in conversation. I didn't think she'd tell Ruby. I forgot... I honestly forgot how sensitive things are on your side. I'm really sorry, Gaurav *bhai*."

Gaurav sighed, but the tension in his shoulders eased. "Please, just be a little more careful next time. How did you even realize that something was wrong with Ruby at my flat?"

"It was around 8 PM," Sidhu began. "We suddenly heard Khushi crying loudly from your flat. At first, we thought she might've hurt herself—kids cry when they get hurt, right? But when 10-15 minutes passed and her screams started sounding more... unsettling, something felt off. I went straight to Khanna uncle's flat and told him everything.

He continued.

"We rang your doorbell—again and again—but no one answered. And Khushi's cries weren't stopping. That's when we decided to break the door down. As soon as we entered, we saw Ruby lying on the floor. Her mouth had white foam coming out—it looked serious. I checked her pulse—she was still breathing, but barely. Without wasting a second, we rushed her to the hospital. I left Khushi at my flat so she wouldn't have to see all this."

Sidhu ended with a sigh.

Gaurav took a deep breath, absorbing everything. He looked at Sidhu and Khanna uncle again, a silent appreciation in his eyes.

"You both saved her," he said simply.

Just then, a voice called out from the reception desk.

"Gaurav sir, please come."

Gaurav walked over.

"Sir, please clear these bills. After that, you're free to take Ruby ma'am home anytime."

"Okay, thank you, ma'am," he said, his tone composed, almost detached.

He spent the next few minutes completing the paperwork, signing forms, and settling the hospital charges. The moment everything was done, he walked back and helped Ruby into the car.

No one spoke.

There were things to say—questions to ask, emotions to process—but silence felt easier.

Ruby sat beside him in the passenger seat, looking out the window. In the back, Khanna uncle, Gajendra, and Sidhu sat quietly, each lost in their own thoughts.

The whole incident had shaken Gaurav to the core. He wasn't just rattled—he was re-evaluating everything.

His hands were steady on the wheel, but inside, he was anything but calm. He kept thinking about that moment in Yogita's flat—how he had stopped himself, drawn the line, and walked away. If he truly had feelings for someone else, if even a sliver of betrayal had existed, he might have lost Ruby forever.

And then, like a memory flashing through windshield glass, came that night in Mussoorie. Even then, when emotions were charged and Ruby was vulnerable, he had chosen restraint. Twice now, he'd faced temptation—and twice, he'd stepped back.

Yet amidst the chaos, a quiet thread of comfort ran through him. Ruby had seen it. She had owned her mistake. Maybe now, the endless suspicion, the short temper, the overthinking—it might ease. Maybe this was the turning point their relationship needed.

After some time, they finally reached home.

The society had gotten wind of what had happened. Whispers had spread, theories had formed. As Gaurav stepped out of his car, he could feel the eyes on him—the stares, the hushed conversations behind closed doors.

But he was unfazed. The gossip, the judgment—none of it mattered anymore. With effortless ease, he ignored it all and walked straight inside.

A carpenter was already fixing the broken door. Inside, Khushi was playing with Sheetal, Gajendra's wife.

*****

The next day, Gaurav walked into the office, carrying his usual carefree attitude. It had been around fourteen days since he started serving his notice period, and he was in a relaxed, almost playful mood. As always, he arrived at 10:20 AM.

As he settled into his seat, his eyes briefly caught Sunny, sitting in the last seat of his row. Head down, hunched over his laptop, almost as if trying to disappear. Gaurav chose to ignore him. He unzipped his laptop bag, ready to start his day.

Before he could even take his laptop out, HR called him into the conference room.

Drishti, the HR executive, didn't waste time. "Gaurav, you've been coming late every day. And you've been taking leaves without informing us beforehand. You need to follow office rules. Please start coming on time."

Gaurav leaned back in his chair, his tone effortless, cool. "Look, ma'am, I have a personal life too. I go to the gym in the morning, so sometimes I get delayed. And leaves? They can't always be planned. Some family issues come up unexpectedly, and when they do, I need to take a leave immediately. These kinds of issues don't come with a schedule. So yes, I might come late again, and yes, I might take an unplanned leave in the future too. You can deduct my salary accordingly, calculate it however you want. But this is how I'm going to continue."

His words were calm, clear, and unwavering. There was no apology—just a statement of fact.

Drishti hadn't expected this kind of response. She had called the meeting to enforce office rules, expecting pushback but not this level of unapologetic clarity. She knew the company demanded discipline, but deep down, she also understood—office pressure was stealing a lot from her too.

"As you wish, sir," she said, her voice neutral, hiding the conflict within.

The meeting wrapped up in just five minutes. No long discussions, no unnecessary arguments. Gaurav walked out, as calm as he had entered, unfazed by the rules that once dictated his routine. His priorities had shifted, and for the first time, he wasn't letting anyone else define them.

Gaurav met Kundan in the morning, discussed a few tasks, and then took a short coffee break.

During lunch, he sat with Yogita and Kapil, but Sunny was nowhere to be seen.

"Gaurav, is everything okay at home?" Yogita asked.

"For now, yeah," Gaurav replied casually.

Kapil pulled out his phone, flipping through some pictures from their Mussoorie trip—Sunny was in a few of them.

"Why didn't Sunny join us for lunch?" Gaurav asked.

"He's scared," Kapil smirked. "He met me earlier today and said, 'I can't face Gaurav and Yogita. I think I'll have to quit my job.'"

Yogita scoffed. "He ran into me too, down at Chotu's shop in the morning. Held his ears, apologized for all the Mussoorie drama."

Gaurav raised an eyebrow. "So, you forgave him?"

"No. In fact, I was even angrier," she replied bluntly.

Gaurav exhaled, shaking his head slightly. "Hmm. Anyway, I've got two job interviews today."

"Oh? So, have you prepared well?" Yogita asked.

"Not really. I'll just say what I know," Gaurav said, leaning back, completely unbothered.

"Alright, best of luck," Yogita and Kapil said in unison.

Lunch break ended, and everyone returned to their seats.

Gaurav put on his headphones, walked into the conference room, and attended both interviews.

Neither went particularly well. Both companies called him back almost instantly, saying he hadn't been selected.

Gaurav hadn't expected this.

Still, he sat back in his chair, opened his laptop, and started applying to more companies.

A craving kicked in. Gaurav needed a smoke.

He got up from his seat and casually strolled toward Sunny. The moment he reached him, Sunny shot up from his chair, startled—his fear was evident in his face.

"Come to the terrace. Let's have a cigarette," Gaurav said, his tone easy, almost nonchalant.

Sunny's mind was racing. *What if he pushes me off the terrace? What if this is some kind of revenge?* He hesitated.

"No, no... I don't feel like it right now."

Gaurav smirked, placing a firm hand on Sunny's shoulder. "Come on."

Sunny had no choice. It wasn't worth the embarrassment of refusing in front of everyone. If he stayed back, he risked looking weak—worse, he feared a public scene. Reluctantly, he walked out with Gaurav.

Moments later, they were on the terrace.

Gaurav lit a cigarette, took a long drag, and exhaled slowly—watching the smoke dissolve into the air. Then, without a word, he handed the cigarette to Sunny.

Sunny stared at it, unsure. He took it anyway, inhaled cautiously, then passed it back.

"Why are you scared of me? You're even thinking about quitting your job because of me. Tell me-why?" Gaurav asked, his voice calm but firm.

Sunny didn't respond.

"Speak up," Gaurav said again, this time exhaling a slow stream of smoke.

Sunny hesitated, then finally admitted, "I told your wife about you... because of me, she ended up in the hospital."

Gaurav nodded slightly, taking in the words without any visible reaction. "Listen, bro. I'm not angry about that. You did what you did to take revenge, I get it. But my wife should've known better than to trust an outsider so blindly. So, I'm not mad at you for that."

Sunny looked at him, completely stunned.

"And as for what happened with Yogita—that was just you being drunk. You got beaten up for it, lesson learned. But understand this—if you ever pull something like that again, whether it's with Yogita or anyone else, I'll beat you up again. Simple as that."

Sunny stood frozen, barely believing what he was hearing. Then, suddenly, he grabbed Gaurav in a tight hug.

"I'm so sorry, bro. I've been such a terrible person," Sunny said, tears streaming down his face.

Gaurav chuckled, patting his back. "Are you crazy? What's all this drama? Come on, let's grab a coffee before I head home."

The tension dissolved as they walked to the cafeteria. Over cups of coffee, they talked—really talked.

"When's your next interview?" Sunny asked, leaning back in his chair.

"Tomorrow. Two interviews. Let's see how it goes," Gaurav said, sounding calm but thoughtful.

Sunny nodded. "Best of luck in advance, bro. Hope you crack at least one!"

"Thanks," Gaurav smiled. He appreciated the encouragement but knew that interviews were unpredictable. You prepare, you hope, and then you wait for fate to play its cards.

Thirty, maybe forty minutes later, they returned to their seats. For the first time in days, there was a smile on Sunny's face.

Gaurav picked up his bag, stretched slightly, and walked out. It was time to go home.

CHAPTER NINE

BETWEEN REJECTIONS AND RELATIVES

Gaurav was preparing for his interviews, scrolling through solutions to past interview questions on the internet. He knew confidence was important, but so was knowledge. No matter how self-assured he felt, he couldn't afford to be underprepared.

Two interviews were lined up—one at 11 AM and the second at 2 PM. He had already faced rejection twice. He had felt the sting of those "*We regret to inform you...*" emails, but he had made peace with it. This time, he wasn't nervous. He was calm, collected. It wasn't about proving anything to anyone anymore—it was just another step forward.

His preparation was almost complete. He glanced at the clock—11 AM was just a few minutes away. Picking up his laptop, he walked towards the conference room, settling in front of the screen. He adjusted his hair, straightened his collar. Appearance mattered—first impressions could tilt the odds.

The interview started. Some questions were straightforward, others... not so much. He answered what he could. Some responses came effortlessly; others had him pausing, searching for words. A tough one caught him off guard—he took a second, exhaled, then answered, hoping his logic would hold up.

"We'll let HR reach out with the results," the interviewers said before signing off.

12 PM. His phone buzzed.

Rejection.

Again.

Gaurav put the phone down, ran his hand through his hair, leaned back. He didn't sigh, didn't react. It wasn't unexpected. And somehow, it didn't feel as bad as before.

Gaurav sat back, staring at his laptop screen, replaying the interview in his mind. The answers, the pauses, the expressions of the panel—every detail ran through his head like a slow-motion sequence. He wasn't panicking, but the thought of going through the whole process again in another hour wasn't exactly pleasant either. Same formalities, same interrogation-style questioning. He exhaled, shaking off the tension.

Just then, his phone rang. He glanced at the screen—Ruby.

Great. More distraction.

He picked up the call, rubbing his temples. "Yes, what's up?"

"You remember, right? We have to go to Gurugram today for Gajendra *Bhai's* anniversary," Ruby reminded him.

Gaurav sighed, running a hand through his hair. "Oh right. Good you reminded me. I'll take a half-day and come home, then we'll leave in the evening."

"Okay. By the way, how was the interview?"

"Not great. Rejected. Again."

"I've been telling you—take back your resignation. You're making a mistake." Her voice had that familiar edge, half frustration, half concern.

"Not this again, Ruby. I'll handle it. I'll be home by two." With that, he hung up, shaking his head.

Just as he put the phone down, Yogita walked over to his desk.

"Hey Gaurav, how did it go?" she asked, her voice carrying an unmistakable warmth.

"Not great. Rejected." His tone was calm, unaffected.

"It's okay, next one's at 1 PM, right?"

"Yeah."

"Alright then, make sure you give this one properly. Come on, let's grab a coffee."

A few minutes of conversation and caffeine later, he felt lighter. Not excited, not hopeful—just... neutral. Which was good enough.

1 PM was creeping up. Time for another interview. The interview went better this time—no fumbling, no awkward silences. But now he has to wait for HR's call. The moment of judgment.

It was almost 2 PM when Gaurav walked over to Kundan's desk.

"Sir, I'll be leaving in a few minutes. Need a half-day today," he said, his tone easy, composed.

Kundan glanced up from his screen, sizing him up for a second. "Something urgent?"

"Yeah, family function. I'll wrap up pending work tomorrow."

"Come with me to the conference room," Kundan said, and both of them walked into the conference room.

Kundan leaned back in his chair, arms crossed. "Gaurav, dedication is needed everywhere. Look at others—some are managers, some are leaders. If you take responsibility, you can lead. And if you lead, you can become a manager. Whether you stay in this company or move to another, you will have to work with responsibility."

Gaurav sighed, waiting. He already knew where this was headed.

"To achieve success, you have to work day and night. Be serious. If you don't work properly, there will be no salary increment in any company. You're in your notice period, but if your performance isn't up to the mark, your release might get delayed, or worse—you may get a bad remark on your release letter."

"If you want to talk friendly, I'll tell you something," Gaurav said, his voice calm but firm. "You are stuck in a cycle, unable to see beyond it. You assume that responsibility equals progress, but that's a narrow way of looking at life. The truth is, work and responsibility don't automatically lead to freedom or success. A laborer can take responsibility, a manager can lead, but at the end of the day, they remain bound to a system that doesn't always reward them the way they imagine.

The more responsibility you take, the deeper you get embedded into that system. If leadership was the only factor, everyone who worked hard would be at the top—but that's not how the world works.

I have detached myself from this mindset. And you know what? This **notice period** is the best thing that's happened to me. This job, this place, my notice period—it has freed me mentally. And in that freedom, I see things differently.

Responsibility is not a universal requirement; it's a choice dictated by priorities. Sometimes, stepping back from one responsibility is the only way to focus on what actually matters. And more often than not, those priorities have nothing to do with money but everything to do with life—whether it's happiness, relationships, or something that gives real meaning beyond the office walls."

Gaurav leaned forward slightly, eyes sharp, but his tone unshaken. "Today, my priority is an anniversary function, and I am leaving. It's not neglect—it's perspective. Right now, you see only the first step of life: attachment. You believe staying committed to work is the only way forward. But there's a second step—detachment—and beyond that the third step is :freedom, the ability to think beyond predefined roles. That's where I am. And believe me, there are more steps ahead, but for now, this is enough for you to understand. Maybe someday, when you break out of this mindset, I'll tell you about the other steps. But until then, keep thinking. Now I am leaving, sir."

Gaurav walked out of the room without waiting for a response, and within a few minutes, he was standing at the exit door, waiting for the lift.

After hearing everything, Kundan was confused. He couldn't figure out whether Gaurav was making sense or just talking in circles. His words lingered, unsettling but oddly convincing. Shaking off the thought, Kundan walked straight to Yogita's desk.

"What's the status of the work?" Kundan asked.

"Sir, it's in progress. A few tasks are still pending," Yogita replied.

"I've been warning you for the last two to three weeks that I need this done on time."

"Sir, I'm trying my best," she said, forcing calm into her voice.

"If it's not done by tomorrow, then you'll have to come in on Saturday. And if it's still pending after Saturday, then Sunday too. But I need the work finished by Monday morning. No excuses." Kundan's tone was firm, leaving no room for argument.

Yogita stayed silent. She just nodded, agreeing without a choice. She wanted to tell him that even if she worked through Saturday and Sunday, the task still wouldn't be completed—but she didn't have the courage to say it.

Without another word, Kundan walked back to his seat.

The pressure was overwhelming. Yogita could feel it creeping in, tightening around her like a suffocating rope. She glanced across the floor and spotted Kapil sitting a few desks away.

Kapil could read her face in an instant. Her eyes looked tired, on the verge of tears. He gestured towards the cafeteria.

"Tea?" he mouthed.

She hesitated for a second, then nodded.

Inside the cafeteria, Kapil ordered two cups of tea and slid into the seat across from her.

"What happened? Why do you look so down?" he asked, his voice light but concerned.

"You heard what Kundan said," she replied in a hushed tone.

Kapil exhaled sharply. "Listen, just do whatever you can. Don't overthink it. "

"He told me to work last Saturday too, but I didn't come to the office. And now again, he's asking me to work through the weekend. But I can't, *yaar*. After five days of work, I get exhausted. I need my Saturday and Sunday to rest. I already put in extra hours on weekdays."

Kapil shook his head. "You'll have to come on the weekend. Otherwise, Kundan's going to get even more annoyed."

The waiter placed their tea on the table.

For a few moments, they just sat there, sipping tea, chatting about random things—anything to distract her from the stress building in her mind. After finishing their tea, they walked back to their desks.

As soon as Gaurav reached home, he started playing with Khushi while casually chatting with Ruby.

"What time do we have to leave for the party?" Gaurav asked.

"Six o'clock, so that we reach *Bhaiya's* place by seven," Ruby replied.

"It's already three. You better start getting ready. You'll take at least three hours just for makeup."

"I'm just doing light makeup. Won't take that long."

Ruby, admiring herself in the mirror at the dressing table, suddenly turned to Gaurav. "This Saturday, I'm getting my hair smoothened. You'll have to come with me to the salon. You and Khushi can wait in the reception area while it's done."

"How long will that take?"

"Three to four hours, minimum."

"So basically, my entire day is gone."

"You'll have to do this much at least."

"Fine, but don't ask me to do anything on Sunday. I'm going to start playing cricket regularly. As you know, I've already joined the cricket club and attended 2–3 sessions. Now, I'm turning it into a regular practice routine. I've wanted to for a long time. I want to keep one day of the week just for myself—so I can do whatever I want. Meet friends, swim, play cricket, or maybe sleep all day. But no house chores on that day."

"I could say the same, that I need one day for myself too. But is that even practical?"

"Sure. You're going to the salon on Saturday because you like it. So keep Saturday free for yourself. Do whatever you want. I'll handle Khushi."

"You won't be able to. You can't even handle a job properly. Just sitting around in your notice period."

Gaurav sighed, shaking his head. "Here we go again. Office talk. Job talk." He picked up the remote and switched on the TV. "Let me know when you're ready. I'll get ready in ten minutes."

A cricket match was on. Gaurav leaned back on the couch, eyes fixed on the screen, immersing himself in the game.

Ruby finished getting ready, and by the time they left, it was almost seven.

At the party, Gaurav greeted his brother-in-law with a warm handshake. "*Namaste*, Gajendra *Bhaiya*! Happy Marriage Anniversary. Bhabhi ji, many congratulations to you as well."

Ruby also wished them, then moved on to meet her parents and the rest of the family.

"You guys took forever to reach!" Gajendra remarked.

"You know Delhi NCR traffic, *Bhaiya*. And today's a working day. Evenings are a nightmare on the roads."

"Speaking of work," Gajendra smirked, "You quit your job, right?"

"Not yet. Still serving my notice period."

"Same thing. Few days left now, right?"

"Yeah, around twenty-twenty five days."

"And I heard you haven't even found another job yet. Quit first, worry later?"

"I'll find something, *Bhaiya*. Let's enjoy the party."

"I'm serious, Gaurav. Once you have a family, quitting a job just like that is not a smart move."

Just then, Gajendra's wife, Sheetal, walked over. "Gaurav ji, you should visit us more often. We never get to see you."

Gaurav smiled. "Time was the issue, Bhabhi ji. But now, time is no problem. I'll come more often with Ruby."

"Of course, now you have plenty of time. Notice period and all," Sheetal quipped sarcastically.

Gaurav's phone suddenly rang—except it didn't. He pretended it did. "Excuse me, *Bhaiya*. Office call." He grabbed his phone and walked away, putting some distance between himself and the conversation.

Cake cutting happened, followed by dinner. The evening went smoothly.

As Gaurav and Ruby made their way to the exit, Gaurav's father-in-law placed a hand on his shoulder and gestured for him to walk alongside him.

"*Beta*, if there's a problem, talk to us. We'll figure something out together. But quitting a job just like that isn't the right approach. Every married person faces challenges—that doesn't mean they leave their job."

Gaurav listened patiently, nodding slightly. "I'll think about it, *Sasur ji*. We're getting late now. We should head home." He folded his hands in respect, touched his feet, and walked towards the car.

Ruby and Khushi were already seated inside.

"The food was amazing at the party, right?" Ruby asked.

Gaurav was driving, his eyes fixed on the road. Without looking at her, he replied, "Yeah, it was good. But your entire family seems more worried about my job than anything else. Everyone was after me. I could've replied harshly, but I thought, what's the point? They'll just get upset, and then you'll be in a bad mood too. So I just listened."

"They're just concerned about you. What's wrong with that?" Ruby made a face.

"They're not concerned. They're making fun of me. People just need something to gossip about. No one actually cares. They just found a guy they can throw unsolicited advice and lectures at."

"You think everyone is useless. Especially my family," Ruby said, annoyed.

Silence filled the car for a few moments.

"Tell me something," Gaurav said finally. "In my journey so far—my studies, my job struggles, marriage, and now reaching thirty-five—who has played the biggest role? Like, who has influenced my life the most?"

Ruby thought for a second. "Your parents."

"No."

"Then I don't know."

"The biggest role in my life has been played by me. I reached here because of my own thoughts, my own struggles. Other people contribute maybe five to seven percent, in some situations. Parents play a role in the early years, but the moment a child starts understanding things, he makes his own decisions. And from then on, his life is shaped by him, not by anyone else."

"Okay... and what's the point of this long lecture?"

"It means that since I've brought myself this far, I'll take myself forward too. So your family doesn't need to give me advice."

"Talking to you is pointless," Ruby muttered.

"You're right," Gaurav replied calmly, eyes fixed on the road.

Silence again.

"By the way," Ruby broke the quiet, "*Bhabhi* is going shopping at Sarojini Market on Sunday, so I'm going with her. Just letting you know—you'll have to keep Khushi at home. Or you can come along, and we can take her with us."

Gaurav sighed. "What did I say earlier? That I need either Saturday or Sunday just for myself, without any responsibilities. So either don't go to the parlor on Saturday, or don't go to Sarojini Market on Sunday."

"I've already told *Bhabhi* I'm going shopping. I have to go." Ruby was firm.

"Fine then. I'll keep Saturday free. You can go to the market on Sunday and get your hair smoothened at the same time. The entire day will be yours."

Ruby stared out the window, arms folded, lips pursed. "You never listen to me, Gaurav. It's always about you. Your weekend, your peace, your alone time."

Gaurav kept his eyes on the road, one hand steady on the steering wheel. "Right. Because fighting with me in a moving vehicle is the best way to prove you care."

"Oh, please," she snapped, turning to him. "I'm the one who's always adjusting. You've suddenly discovered this 'me time' concept and now the entire household should bend backwards?"

He sighed. "I'm asking for one day, Ruby. One quiet, responsibility-free day. That's all."

"And I'm asking for four hours at a salon and some time at Sarojini with *Bhabhi*. Is that too much to expect?"

Gaurav's tone sharpened as he glanced at her. "You always twist it into a fight. Always looking for the smallest spark."

She leaned closer. "I started the fight? Really?"

He smirked, eyes on the road. "Of course not. You never start them. They just mysteriously combust around you."

Ruby sat back, anger bubbling now. "You think I can't do things alone? Fine. I'll go for hair smoothing on Saturday. Market on Sunday. Both days. And no, I don't need you for anything."

"That's all I've been saying. Go on your own," he replied, calm but cold.

The car went silent. Only the hum of the engine filled the space between them.

Gaurav turned on the FM radio. It was late at night, and old songs were playing.

Both of them were lost in their own thoughts. Khushi was asleep in the back seat.

Joining, But on My Terms

"Shivani, your project is finished, right?" As soon as Shivani entered the office, she was passing by Kundan when he suddenly spoke up.

"Good morning, sir. Yes, sir," Shivani responded.

"I'm sending an email right now. I'll mention that you need to take the project handover from Gaurav."

"Okay, sir."

"He's either leaving early or taking days off, this way, his current project won't be completed on time. And the handover for the other projects will get delayed too. So take the handover carefully and make sure everything is clear."

"Sure, sir."

"By the way, don't you feel that Gaurav has changed a lot lately?"

"Yeah, sir. I feel the same. He's even influencing some colleagues."

"You've spoken to him, right?"

"Yes, once. He was talking about attachment, detachment, and freedom."

"So what do you think? Was he making sense?"

"Honestly, sir, his point was valid. But quitting a job is a huge risk. I wouldn't take it."

"Hmm. Alright. Get back to work now."

Kundan leaned back in his chair, lost in thought.

"I'm attached to this job—that's true. But how do I detach? Does detachment mean quitting outright? Does freedom come only after leaving a job? No, no. I can't quit. I have a wife, kids, elderly parents. It's not that simple.

But still... I do wish for a different life. Traveling, living freely. Life has passed by, and I never got time for myself. Maybe I should talk to Gaurav about all this."

Just then, Yogita entered and broke his thoughts.

"Good morning, sir," she said.

"Good morning, Yogita," Kundan replied absently.

Yogita expected him to ask for project updates and maybe even scold her about deadlines. But surprisingly, he remained quiet, lost in his thoughts again.

One by one, the staff arrived, greeted him, and settled into their seats. Kundan snapped back to reality.

He said,"Gaurav, I've sent you an email about the handover. Sit with Shivani and start handing over the work." His voice wasn't as authoritative as usual—but still, he retained some presence as a manager.

"Sure, sir," Gaurav replied. He was scrolling through his emails, checking details about upcoming interviews.

Since morning, Kundan had been consumed by one thought—employees were taking unwanted leaves, and he needed to find a way to stop it. His mind kept churning, plotting different tactics to extract work from people, often crossing the line between management and manipulation.

Just then, Kapil strolled over to Gaurav's desk.

"Gaurav, I have something to ask you. Want to grab a cup of tea?" Kapil said.

Both got up and walked toward the cafeteria.

"What will you have? Tea or coffee?" Kapil asked.

"Coffee," Gaurav said.

A few minutes later, a steaming cup of tea and coffee sat on the table.

"I'm confused about something," Kapil admitted. "I understand attachment. But does detachment simply mean quitting a job?"

Gaurav took a slow sip of his coffee and leaned forward slightly.

"Detachment doesn't mean quitting your job," Gaurav explained patiently, stirring his coffee. "Try to understand it deeply. Detachment means treating something as less important to your happiness. If something is stopping you from doing what truly matters to you, then it has power over you. That's why stepping back or lowering its priority is real detachment."

He leaned back, choosing his words carefully. "Let me give you an example. Suppose you drink alcohol every day, and now you're addicted. If this addiction is making your life better, fine. But if it's ruining everything—your happiness, your relationships, your health—then you're attached to it in the wrong way. You need to detach. Simple."

Kapil frowned. "But if I don't prioritize my job, how will I grow in my career?"

Gaurav smiled, his voice calm and assured. "Then you're making a mistake. Career growth is just greed. Money will come, but if you invest all your time in it, later you'll say—'My life is full of stress, my family isn't happy, I can't enjoy life'—and all that. And say you do grow. You'll keep getting promoted, keep working, and one day retire as a bald old man wondering where all your time went. Then the regret will hit—you spent your whole life chasing something, and your real desires were left behind."

Kapil exhaled, nodding slowly. "Hmm. Makes sense. So we can stay detached even while working, right?"

"Exactly," Gaurav said, adjusting his watch casually. "It's all about keeping priorities in check. If your company tells you not to come from tomorrow, just say—'Why tomorrow? I can quit today itself.' You should be that mentally strong, that detached."

Kapil laughed, shaking his head. "Got it. I'll think about it properly." He took a sip, then changed the topic. "By the way, did you get selected anywhere else?"

"Not yet," Gaurav chuckled. "The hunt is on."

Their coffee was finished, and as they talked, they both walked back to their seats. The conversation lingered in the air, making Kapil rethink a few things. Gaurav, on the other hand, seemed relaxed—almost as if he had already figured out what mattered.

It was 11 AM when Gaurav's phone rang.

"Hi Gaurav, I'm Gauri from PHCL Technologies. Congratulations! You've been selected in the interview. Your salary, working hours, and other details are mentioned in the email. Let me know if you have any questions," she said in a professional yet friendly tone.

"Thanks a lot," Gaurav replied, a small smile playing on his lips. "I'll check the email and get back to you."

He hung up and immediately opened his inbox, scrolling through until he found the email. His excitement was undeniable—this was the sixth interview he had attended, and finally, he had cleared one. He started reading the terms carefully, one by one:-

- CTC : please find attached PDF

- Office timings: 9 AM to 6 PM.

- Arriving late three times will be considered a half-day.

- Leaving early three times will also be considered a half-day.

- Sick leave should be informed at least a day in advance.

- Annual leave requires a 15-day prior notice.

- Sudden leave will be considered unpaid.

- Notice period: 3 months.

- Misbehavior with seniors can lead to immediate termination.

As he went through the conditions, the happiness on his face slowly faded into contemplation. The carefree ease of his notice period felt like a distant dream, now replaced with the reality of another corporate cage. He sighed, leaning back in his chair. Was he really ready to walk into another rigid system?

No. Not this time.

"If they have their terms and conditions, then I will have mine too," he thought, a newfound determination settling in. He wasn't going to get trapped again. If a company wanted him, they'd have to accept him on his own terms.

With that, he grabbed a notepad and started listing down his own conditions. A few minutes later, satisfied with what he had written, he picked up his phone and dialed Gauri's number.

This time, the conversation was going to be different.

"Hi Gauri, good morning. Gaurav this side," he said, leaning back in his chair.

"Good morning, Gaurav. Hope you've gone through the email. Are you satisfied with the terms?" Gauri asked politely.

"Gauri , I have a few conditions," Gaurav said, his tone composed but firm. "Please note them down. If the company can agree to these, then let me know."

"Alright. Tell me, I'm listening," Gauri replied, her fingers ready on the keyboard.

"Number one—I'll work 8 hours a day. Not 9, not 10—just 8. And those 8 hours? They can begin any time I want. Could be early morning, late night, or even after dinner. My day, my clock."

He paused for a second, then continued, "Second, I'll work 22 days in a month. And I'll choose which ones. If I feel like working on a Sunday and taking Tuesday off, I will. Your calendar won't decide my life."

Gauri hummed in response, signaling that she was noting everything down.

"Third," Gaurav went on, "When I'm on leave, I'm gone. Off the grid. No calls, no pings, no 'urgent request' messages. If I'm off, treat it like I disappeared."

He adjusted his watch, his voice steady and assured. "Fourth, Every year, my salary will grow by 20%. Non-negotiable. No rating drama or manager mood swings—just math."

Gauri's typing slowed down a bit, but she didn't interrupt.

"And fifth—If I arrive late or leave early, deal with it. I'll still complete my 8 hours. Might work from home, or from a café, or at midnight. You'll get the work. I'll get peace."

There was silence on the call for a moment.

"Gauri, are you still there?" Gaurav asked.

"Yes, Gaurav. I'm listening. I've noted down your conditions," she finally replied. "I will check with my seniors and get back to you."

"Great. Thanks," he said, ending the call.

Gaurav put his phone down and exhaled. He knew this was a bold move—most people wouldn't even think of negotiating terms like this. He wasn't looking for just another job. He wanted freedom, clarity, and control over his time.

Whatever happened next, he wasn't going to compromise.

Shivani walked up to Gaurav's seat.

"Hi, Gaurav. How are you?" she asked, flashing a tired smile.

"I'm good. What about you? The last time we met was during the office badminton tournament. You've vanished since then," Gaurav said, leaning back casually.

"Oh, don't ask. It's been terrible. I just finished a project yesterday. I've been losing my mind over it for the past six months. After that tournament, I barely got any time."

"Well, now it's done, relax a bit."

"I wish ! Even though it's delivered, if there are issues, I'll be stuck again. And now I have to take the handover of your projects. The deadline for completing your tasks will eventually be my headache."

"Hmmm. That's true. Find a way to deal with it. Or just start loving what you do."

"By the way, why are you quitting? I heard you don't even have an offer letter from another company yet."

"Didn't feel like wasting my life here. Thought I'd do something different. Can't afford to let my time slip away like this."

"Oh. Well, you can do anything, Gaurav. We all know that. Now, brief me about all your projects."

"First, coffee?"

"Fine."

Gaurav and Shivani got up from their seats and headed toward the cafeteria.

From a distance, Yogita watched them, her stomach twisting with jealousy. She liked Gaurav but always made sure never to let it show.

She waited for a few minutes, but her patience ran out. Finally, she walked into the cafeteria. She scanned the place, pretending to be casual, then spotted him. Picking up a cup of tea, she walked up to him.

"Hi, Gaurav," she said.

"Hello, Yogita. How's it going?" Gaurav asked.

"I'm fine. But clearly, you've got a new friend now. Hardly notice anyone else," she said, eyeing Shivani with mock irritation.

"Oh, come on. She's not a new friend. She's my badminton partner. We played doubles together last year."

"Hi, Shivani," Yogita said, extending a hand.

"Hello, Yogita," Shivani replied, shaking it.

Just then, Kapil and Sunny walked in. Everyone exchanged handshakes and sat around the table, except Yogita and Sunny.

They didn't say hello. No handshake. Nothing. The moment their eyes met, *the night in Mussoorie* flashed back in their minds. It was one of those moments that couldn't be undone. Too much had happened. A simple handshake wouldn't fix things.

Even so, all of them sat together around the table.

Sipping their tea and coffee, conversation flowed. Then suddenly, Gaurav's phone rang. As soon as he pulled it out of his pocket, the chatter stopped. He answered.

"Hello, Gaurav. It's Gauri."

"Yes, Gauri. Tell me," he said calmly.

"The company didn't accept your terms. Sorry, we won't be able to hire you on your terms."

"No problem. Thanks for letting me know. Anything else?" Gaurav's tone was neutral, completely unaffected.

There was silence on the other end for a moment. Then, Gauri spoke again.

"There is one thing I wanted to ask."

"Go ahead."

"Nobody has ever asked for terms like this before. To be honest, I wish I could work under similar conditions too. But that's never an option. How do you have so much confidence?"

Gaurav exhaled, looking at the steam rising from his coffee. His voice remained composed.

"It's not confidence. It's just respecting myself—without manipulation, without justification. You can't get it. Nobody gets it. Because everyone is busy asking someone else how to get it. The ones who truly have it never asked how to get it. They just woke up one day knowing."

Gauri was silent for a moment. Then she sighed.

"Hmm... So I need to ask myself what I really want. It's starting to make sense. I'm saving your number. I'll connect with you on WhatsApp. I'm sad the company couldn't hire you, but I'm happy I found someone like you. Please keep in touch."

"Sure. Thanks. Bye."

The call ended.

Yogita, Shivani, Kapil, and Sunny had heard everything. They glanced at Gaurav with a new sense of respect.

"Guys, my engagement's the day after tomorrow," Kapil announced, excitement flickering behind his glasses. "You're all invited. It's at the Blue Rose Hotel in Ghaziabad."

There was a beat of silence.

"You sneaky bastard!" Gaurav said, grinning. "Planning a whole engagement and didn't drop even a hint?"

"*Arrey yaar*," Yogita chimed in, "I don't think I'll get leave. The manager's already breathing down my neck."

"Who all have you invited?" Gaurav asked.

"I've told 8–10 friends from the office," Kapil replied.

Sunny shrugged, "Can't say anything for sure. Don't think everyone will get time off. You know how it is—deadlines, clients, approvals."

Gaurav leaned back, his tone shifting. "I'm definitely going. Engagements, weddings—these are once-in-a-lifetime events. We spend so much time chasing targets that we forget the people who'll actually cry when we're gone. Learn to set priorities, guys. Strengthen relationships. Don't cling to the office so tightly that you lose sight of the real world outside."

"You're right, Gaurav," Yogita said, her voice carrying a trace of regret. "Last year, one of my close friends got married. But I couldn't attend—office work kept me tied up. And honestly, I still feel bad about it. Every time we talk, she makes sure to remind me—'You didn't even have time to come to my wedding.'"

She paused, then smiled, a little more certain. "But this time, I'm definitely coming, Kapil."

Everyone else had also agreed to attend the engagement. It was clear—Gaurav's words were leaving an impression on them all.

In a few minutes.

The conversation slowed down. After a few minutes later, One by one, they all got up and started heading back to their desks.

Shivani walked back with Gaurav, carrying her laptop. Soon, they settled down and began discussing project details, line by line.

CHAPTER ELEVEN

WHEN EVERY MEETING FEELS LIKE A WARNING

It was Monday—every employee's least favorite day. After two days of fun and relaxation, the thought of returning to work felt unbearable. Some employees had even worked through Saturday and Sunday due to tight project deadlines, but Yogita wasn't one of them. She had ignored Kundan's request to work over the weekend, which meant—without a doubt—her project was delayed.

She stepped into the office cautiously, her eyes lowered, scanning the floor as if looking for something invisible. Her mind drifted back to school days—the way she'd pray that the math teacher wouldn't show up when she hadn't done her homework. *"Maybe he'll fall sick, maybe he has a family emergency, or maybe—just maybe—he'll have a sudden heart attack,"* she had thought back then. Today, the same nervous energy gripped her.

As she walked towards her seat, something felt off. The floor looked emptier than usual. She lifted her eyes and scanned the workspace properly—she wasn't imagining things. A lot of seats were vacant. She caught sight of Kapil sitting a few desks away and gestured toward him.

"Kundan?" she asked softly.

Kapil simply pointed toward the conference room.

Yogita placed her bag on her seat and walked over to Kapil's desk.

"Hi Kapil, why is everyone in the conference room?"

"Hey Yogita. The Branch Manager is here. There's been a meeting going on since morning," Kapil said, looking half-bored, half-exhausted.

Yogita hesitated. "And Gaurav? Haven't seen him around."

Kapil smirked. "You think Gaurav comes on time? He'll be here by 11. It's only 10:15."

Yogita nodded knowingly. "Yeah, true. He's moving on his own terms these days."

She headed back to her seat and began checking her pending work, feeling a little restless.

Meanwhile, the atmosphere inside the conference room was tense.

"Kundan, why is it that only your department's employees are taking leaves so frequently?" General Manager Vipul Bajaj's voice was sharp. "Last Monday, 12 out of 35 employees were absent. Today, it's 10! For the past few weeks, I've been seeing reports—delayed projects, low workforce, things falling behind in your branch!"

Kundan cleared his throat. "Sir, there's a lot of work pressure these days. Maybe that's why people are taking leaves—to escape the load. And honestly, one more reason could be Gaurav. I've heard from others that his words are influencing his colleagues. But it's fine... his notice period will be over soon anyway."

Vipul slammed his hand on the table. "Shut up. If there's so much work pressure, people should be coming in regularly. Not taking leaves left and right!"

Vipul let out a frustrated sigh. "How are you approving so many leave requests? Shouldn't you be keeping a check?"

Kundan tried explaining, "Sir, I rejected five leave applications, but employees are still taking off on their own. And when we ask them why they didn't come, they just say, 'Deduct salary if you want.' And another major reason was Kapil's engagement—many people were off that day."

Vipul shook his head, looking even more irritated.

Inside the conference room, ten associate leads and team leads sat in tense silence, facing Vipul Bajaj's sharp questioning. The air was heavy, the kind that makes people shift uncomfortably in their chairs. Nobody wanted to be the next target of Vipul's frustration.

"I need reports from all the leads by evening," Vipul's voice cut through the silence. "How many projects are delayed? And also, give me a list of those employees who said, 'Cut our salary' and didn't turn up today."

His words hung in the air for a moment. Heads nodded in silent agreement. Nobody dared to argue. There was no point. Orders were orders.

Vipul sighed, ran a hand through his hair, and strode out of the room, his irritation evident. The remaining leads exchanged brief glances before making their way back to their desks.

Yogita noticed Gaurav finally walking in—calm, unbothered, like the chaos in the office didn't concern him.

"Ah, the star of late arrivals has arrived," she said with a smirk.

Gaurav chuckled, unhurriedly placing his bag on the chair. "Time is relative, Yogita."

She rolled her eyes. "Yeah, yeah, Einstein. The branch manager is here, by the way. Big meeting, big drama."

Gaurav leaned back in his chair, unimpressed. "Sounds exciting. Let me know if they start distributing awards for attendance."

Yogita laughed but quickly focused on her laptop. The office had a long day ahead.

Kundan's voice was sharp and authoritative. "Everyone, follow me to the conference room."

A few employees exchanged nervous glances. The tense atmosphere had already taken a toll on them. Nobody wanted to be dragged into another round of questioning.

Gaurav, however, was unfazed. He wasn't bothered by the tension, nor did he care about the chaos around him. He was simply counting down the days, waiting for his exit.

He stood up casually and asked, "Sir, me too?"

Kundan's irritation was evident. "Yes, you too," he snapped.

Gaurav shrugged, unfazed as ever. He wasn't going to fight it. If nothing else, the conference room drama might entertain him for a while.

The conference room was packed. The tension in the air was palpable as Kundan entered and slammed the door shut.

"I've been observing for the past few weeks," Kundan began, his voice sharp. "Too many employees have been taking frequent leaves. And when I checked, none of them had any emergencies. They're taking time off just for fun!"

A few employees exchanged uneasy glances. No one wanted to be called out.

"If this continues, I will have to initiate mass firing. So, I suggest everyone stop being careless and focus on work!"

The room fell silent. The weight of Kundan's words hung heavily.

"Projects are getting delayed, and our company's relationships with clients are suffering. Senior management is furious. Consider this your final warning—start taking your work seriously."

He picked up his glass, took a slow sip of water, and placed it back on the table. His gaze swept over the room. "If anyone has personal problems affecting their work, speak now. If you have questions, ask them."

Silence.

Kundan sighed. "Fine. If no one has anything to say, get back to work. Yogita, you stay."

Chairs scraped against the floor as employees got up and left the room.

Gaurav was the first to step out, a smirk playing on his lips. He knew that people were slowly adopting his approach—not taking the job too seriously. But he also understood the risk. If people were making informed decisions, that was fine. But if they were just blindly following him, they might end up in trouble.

He reached his seat just as Shivani arrived—the colleague he had to hand over work to. He had barely settled in when he saw Yogita approaching.

One look at her face, and it was obvious—she had been crying.

Without hesitation, Gaurav logged off his laptop and walked over to her desk.

"Come on. Let's get some coffee," he said casually.

Yogita sat still, silent.

He gently pulled her up and led her to the cafeteria.

Once they arrived, he gestured toward a chair. "Sit."

She obeyed without a word.

"Alright, what's wrong? Your face looks miserable," Gaurav asked.

"Kundan," she muttered.

"What did he say?"

"He humiliated me. Badly. Told me my only focus is food, that I've gained weight, and I should start focusing on work instead." Her voice broke, and fresh tears rolled down her cheeks.

Gaurav grabbed a tissue and handed it to her.

"And then he said I must have spent my weekend with my boyfriend, which is why I didn't come to work," she added, wiping her tears.

Gaurav sighed. "Yogita, I've told you before—think about yourself. Don't let this toxic environment ruin your life. Ignore his nonsense. The guy's a workaholic mule," he said, shaking his head.

"I'm resigning today," she declared.

"Listen, quitting isn't always the best solution. You have rent to pay, money to send home, and your own survival to think about. When you came to Noida, you barely had anything. But over time, you built your space, got everything you needed. Right now, your circumstances are controlling you. If you make the wrong move now, you'll only end up hurting yourself. You need to change your situation—step into a new environment. Only then will this pain start to fade. First, try to improve them—then resign," Gaurav explained.

"How do I improve them?"

"Cut down expenses. Reduce the amount you send home for a while. Save up at least six to eight months' worth of funds for yourself. Meanwhile, start looking for another job or a business idea—something you actually want to do. Once you have a safety net, resign. That way, even if you don't find something immediately, you can survive comfortably for six months."

Yogita nodded slowly. "That makes sense." A flicker of hope crossed her face. After a moment, she hesitated. "But why did you resign? Do you have a job lined up? Or some idea?"

"I have no idea what's next," Gaurav admitted. "But I have enough savings to last a year. And I had to take that step. This notice period has given me a different kind of wisdom. I'll tell you about it sometime... But for now, chill and focus on what I said."

"Thanks again. Also, I need to apologize to you."

"For what?"

"For hugging you that day at my place. I got emotional," she admitted.

"It's fine. Happens sometimes. And honestly, there's nothing to apologize for. Guys don't mind when girls hug them," Gaurav said, throwing her a wink.

A faint smile crept onto her face.

"So... should I do it again?" she teased.

"Shut up, idiot," he chuckled.

For a brief moment, Yogita forgot the humiliation she had faced earlier. The tension had eased, the mood lighter. They finished their coffee and returned to their desks, ready to get through the rest of the day.

"Shivani, I have two interviews—one at 3 PM and another at 4 PM. Get as much information about the project as you can now, then I'll leave early," Gaurav said.

"Alright, tell me about the smaller project first. I'm exhausted, man. I shifted rooms yesterday—spent the entire Sunday moving stuff. Didn't get a second to rest," Shivani replied, rubbing her temples.

Gaurav quickly handed over one project, explaining the basic details. By 2 PM, he was out of the office.

He headed straight to his usual tea stall.

"Hello *Chotu*, how's life? One tea and one cigarette," Gaurav said, settling down.

"Bhaiya, haven't seen you in days! Coming to the office less often these days?" *Chotu* asked while grabbing a cigarette pack.

"Yeah, not showing up much. And in ten days, I won't be coming at all."

"Why?" *Chotu* handed him the cigarette .

"I quit. I'm on my notice period now," Gaurav said, lighting his cigarette.

Chotu started pouring tea into the cup from the kettle.

"Okay... so where are you headed next?" *Chotu* asked curiously.

Gaurav exhaled a puff of smoke and took a sip of tea. "No idea yet," he said casually.

They chatted for a while—random conversations about life, work, and nothing in particular. After paying for his tea, Gaurav got up and left.

Since it was daytime, the roads were relatively empty. He reached home in just half an hour.

Gaurav rang the doorbell.

The door opened, and he saw his father standing there. His father had been the one to open it. Gaurav touched his father's feet as a sign of respect, then did the same for his mother, who was sitting on the sofa.

Ruby walked in with a glass of water, but her face clearly showed her irritation. She handed over the glass reluctantly.

"Papa, you came all of a sudden. You didn't even call or message," Gaurav said.

His father's face remained firm. Years of hard work as a tailor had sculpted his personality into someone tough and disciplined. His hair was completely white, his features sharp. His words were always precise, never sugar coated.

"You don't like us visiting?" his father asked.

"No, Papa, that's not what I meant. It's just that if both of us had gone out, you would have found the door locked. Then you'd have called, and we'd have rushed back," Gaurav explained, his tone calm and collected.

"Can we at least let him come inside properly before starting a debate?" His mother interjected from behind.

Gaurav glanced at Ruby's expressions. He understood instantly—she wasn't happy about his parents' sudden arrival.

After changing his clothes, he joined his parents in conversation.

"Did you leave your job?" his mother asked bluntly. "Ruby was telling me you're serving your notice period, and you don't have another job lined up."

"Mom, don't worry. I'll handle everything. I got another job. I appeared for an interview, and they selected me," Gaurav lied effortlessly, just to keep his mother's mind at peace.

"Which company?" Ruby asked, clearly skeptical.

"There is one... I don't remember the name right now," Gaurav answered casually.

It remains unclear why a son sometimes lies to make his mother happy, while a daughter-in-law prefers to tell the truth to make her mother-in-law worried and her husband feel humiliated.

The dinner conversation continued with sharp remarks being exchanged.

Later, as Gaurav entered his room to sleep, he noticed that Ruby was still upset. He picked up Khushi, their daughter, held her close, and played with her for a while. Then he turned to Ruby and asked, "What happened? Why are you so angry?"

"Why did your parents come?," Ruby replied in a clipped tone.

Gaurav opened his eyes again, sighing softly as he turned toward her. "Ruby, they're not here to take over our lives. They're just getting old, yaar. *Thoda sa time, thoda sa pyar*—that's all they want. Khushi gets to spend time with her grandparents, and we get a breather too. It's not a burden... it's a blessing, if we choose to see it that way."

Ruby looked at him skeptically. "And when they start interfering in our decisions—what then? When they begin telling Khushi what to eat, how to dress, how to behave?"

Gaurav smiled faintly, his voice gentle now. "*Tab main bolunga, Ruby. Main unka beta hoon, par tere saath hoon.* Trust me, we'll handle it—together."

Ruby looked at him, her anger softening as his words sank in. Maybe he was right—maybe it wasn't about control or interference, but about family, about moments they'd regret missing later. She let out a small sigh and nodded slowly.

"Okay," she murmured, her voice quieter now. "Let's see how it goes... together."

Gaurav placed Khushi beside him, rested a protective hand on her, and closed his eyes.

Ruby switched off the lights and went to sleep.

CHAPTER TWELVE

MORE THAN A FAREWELL: A STEP TOWARD FREEDOM

Another week had passed. Today was Gaurav's last day at the office. His sixty-day notice period—two long months—had finally come to an end.

He was handing over his last project to Shivani when his phone buzzed. The screen flashed a familiar name—Gauri HR.

Gaurav picked up.

"Hi Gauri," he said, his voice steady and calm.

"Hello, Gaurav! How are you?" Gauri sounded cheerful.

"I'm doing fine. What about you?"

"I'm good too. I've joined another company, AR Group Limited. It's a big company. This company has approximately 55 branches. It operates all over the world. Are you interested in joining?"

Gaurav leaned back in his chair. "Gauri, you know I've got my conditions. Without them, I'm not taking up any job. That's why I've given fifteen interviews so far, but haven't landed anywhere yet."

"You should hear me out," Gauri insisted. "They need someone with five to six years of experience, and they found your profile solid. The salary's great, they are giving you an 80% hike then this salary and they're okay with your conditions."

Gaurav raised an eyebrow. "Really? What exactly did they see in me?"

"Well... I may have hyped you up a little," she admitted with a laugh. "I'm your friend now. This much I can do for you."

Gaurav chuckled. "Thanks."

The very first thought that crossed his mind was to set aside a portion of his salary and build a financial backup for the next 5–7 years. 80% hike means almost double the salary.

That way, he smiled to himself, I could technically stay on "notice period" for the next five years... and still sleep in peace.

"So, when can you join?" Gauri asked.

"Today's my last day here. I can start in four or five days."

"Great! I'll send the offer letter by email."

"Alright. Thanks. Bye."

"Bye!"

Shivani, seated nearby, had heard everything. She turned to Gaurav with a grin.

"Congratulations! You got a new job!"

"Thanks," Gaurav said, still as calm as ever.

Just then, an email popped into his inbox. Turns out, Shivani had received the same one.

"Today is Gaurav's last day. He has been with our company for four years, and we will bid him farewell with a party. All are requested to be available in the conference room at 3 PM for an hour." — From Kundan.

Kundan had sent it to the entire department.

Yogita walked up to Gaurav's desk.

"Let's go get some coffee," she said.

"I'll call Kapil and Sunny too," Gaurav replied, stretching a little before getting up.

All of them headed to the cafeteria.

By now, word had spread—Gaurav had received an offer letter from a new company today itself.

"You finally got a job!" Kapil said.

"Yep, finally," Gaurav nodded.

"So, when's the party?"

"Tomorrow evening. Are you free?"

"For a party? Always!"

"Alright, let's do it tomorrow. I'll take you guys to a bar."

"A bar, huh?" Sunny smirked.

Yogita rolled her eyes. She knew how Sunny behaved after drinking.

For a second, Sunny looked excited, but then he caught Yogita's expression and immediately toned himself down.

Everyone sat back and enjoyed their tea and coffee, trying to soak in the moment. Today was Gaurav's last day. They all felt it—an odd mix of happiness and sadness.

After an hour-long tea break, they returned to their seats.

Kundan had been noticing all this. He finally spoke up.

"Yogita, finish your work and give it to me by tomorrow," he said loudly.

"Yes, sir," Yogita replied in a low voice.

It was obvious—Kundan's irritation had reached its peak. People were still taking unplanned leaves, affecting work. But somewhere, deep down, he was relieved. With Gaurav gone, everyone would be back to focusing on work.

The day was dragging on.

Gaurav himself was eager to wrap things up. He just wanted to hand over his laptop to IT and leave.

Finally, it was 2:50 PM. One by one, people started heading towards the conference room.

*****

The conference room felt emptier than usual. General Manager Vipul Bajaj, Kundan, and HR Drishti sat together on one side, while the remaining employees occupied the other. With so many people on leave, only twenty-five were physically present.

On the wall, a monitor displayed a live Microsoft Teams call—almost 300 employees from other branches had joined online. It was unusual. **No farewell** had ever been conducted on such a large scale. But this wasn't just about bidding farewell to Gaurav.

Kundan, Vipul, and Drishti had a different plan. They weren't just sending him off; they were making a statement to the entire company. **They want to humiliate him to set an example for other employees, ensuring they remain disciplined and focused on their work.**

"This," they wanted to show, "is what happens when someone challenges the system, when someone doesn't conform."

Kundan looked around. "Is everyone here?"

The employees exchanged glances, nodding in confirmation. The room felt quieter than usual, almost subdued.

Just then, the peon walked in. "Sir, how many cold drinks and pizzas should I bring? Please confirm the order."

Kundan pulled out a slip from his pocket—he had already listed everything beforehand. Without saying a word, he handed it over and gestured for the peon to leave.

The peon hurried out, closing the door behind him.

A strange air lingered in the room. Some were genuinely feeling the farewell moment, while others just wanted the event to wrap up quickly so they could return to work.

Gaurav sat calmly, observing everything. He wasn't feeling overly sentimental, nor was he restless. He was detached, yet present—just waiting for things to unfold at their own pace.

The atmosphere in the conference room shifted.

Kundan cleared his throat and spoke up, his voice carrying a mix of formality and underlying resentment.

"So, today's party is to bid farewell to Gaurav. It's been a good four years working with him. Although, let's not forget—recently, he misbehaved, gave threats, took leaves without informing anyone... all signs of an irresponsible and unprofessional person."

A few people exchanged awkward glances. Some lowered their heads, avoiding eye contact.

Gaurav, however, remained composed, his face unreadable. He wasn't going to react.

Kundan continued, his tone carrying a sharp edge.

"One time, I had an urgent delivery for a client. I told Gaurav it was critical and that he needed to come in on Saturday. But he flat-out refused. Because of that, I had to get another employee to sit with me and complete the work over the weekend. Only then did we manage to make the delivery.

Another time, I asked him to stay back a little longer and finish a task—just a few points were left. But he didn't agree. He casually said that it wasn't a big deal if the work wasn't completed today, we could just do it tomorrow. He never really took his responsibilities seriously."

Vipul Bajaj adjusted his posture, his voice steady but pointed.

"It's important to recognize contributions, but it's equally important to acknowledge the negatives. An organization thrives on discipline, on teamwork. We need people who respect its structure. I hope, wherever Gaurav goes next, he understands this better."

A few employees exchanged silent glances. The underlying tension was palpable, hanging in the air like an unspoken truth.

Vipul continued, now turning the conversation toward a specific incident. "There was a time when I had an important meeting with our US client. I asked Gaurav to share the presentation with me. I was supposed to lead the discussion. But he didn't. Instead, he presented it himself."

His words were sharp, laced with disappointment. "He wanted the credit. That's why he kept the presentation to himself, refusing to share it with anyone. Because of that, I felt humiliated in front of the client."

The room remained quiet. A few employees looked down, unsure of how to react. Others kept their eyes on Gaurav, waiting for a response.

But Gaurav? He didn't blink. Didn't shift in his chair. Didn't react at all.

He just listened. Calmly. Detached, yet present.

Kundan leaned forward, his voice sharper this time. "You know, Gaurav, some people leave a company with respect. They build relationships, contribute sincerely, and ensure a smooth transition. And then there are others—people who think they're too smart, who challenge the system, make things difficult, and expect special treatment." His words were heavy with implication.

The room was still. A few employees shifted uncomfortably in their seats.

Vipul Bajaj sighed, crossing his arms. "You had potential, Gaurav. But attitude matters. The way you took leaves, the way you handled things in the last few months—it showed a lack of accountability. Companies don't run on individual whims. They run on discipline and structure."

Drishti, the HR representative, leaned forward slightly, her voice carrying a finality that made the atmosphere even heavier.

"You know, Gaurav, professionalism isn't just about skills—it's about attitude. Over time, we saw a pattern in your behavior. You challenged rules, ignored protocols, and acted as if the company owed you something. That's not how things work in the corporate world."

Drishti continued, picking up another instance to drive her point home.

"Once, I scheduled an interview for a candidate—specifically for Gaurav. But he refused to take it, saying he was busy. Because of that, I had to reschedule it for a week later. And when he finally took the interview, he rejected the candidate. I am certain he did it intentionally."

She paused briefly, letting the words settle before adding another layer.

"And it wasn't just that. There was a complaint from an employee about threats. When I tried to take action, the very next day, the person who had complained withdrew his request, saying everything was 'fine' with Gaurav now. I can't help but feel he pressured them into taking back their complaint."

The peon pushed open the door and placed pizzas and cold drinks on the table. No one moved to open them. The mood in the room had shifted—darker, heavier. Everyone could feel it. Gaurav was one of them, had worked among them for years, and yet, here he was, being torn apart, humiliated repeatedly.

For almost fifty minutes, Kundan, Vipul, and Drishti had taken turns criticizing him—not directly, but masked under formal statements. The air was tense; some people looked uncomfortable, while others simply stayed silent, letting it all unfold.

Kundan finally leaned back in his chair and turned towards Gaurav. His tone was casual, but there was an edge to it.

"Gaurav, if you have anything to say, you can speak now. You've got ten minutes. After that, we have project deliveries to take care of. You, of course, wouldn't be bothered about that anymore—you're leaving."

The words weren't an invitation. They were bait.

Kundan, Vipul, and Drishti never intended to let Gaurav have the floor. But last month, Gaurav had spoken about attachment and detachment—about freedom. His words had lingered in Kundan's mind.

Maybe that's why, for just a few minutes, Kundan was willing to let him speak.

He crossed his arms, looking at Gaurav. "Go ahead, Gaurav. What do you want to say to everyone?"

All eyes turned to him. Some with curiosity, some with unease, and some—like Shivani and Kapil—with quiet anticipation.

Gaurav adjusted his posture slightly, resting his hands on the table. He wasn't rattled. He wasn't bitter. He just took a breath, glanced around the room, and then, with a calm certainty, he spoke.

"Kundan, if you guys don't have the time, that's perfectly fine. I won't say a word. But if I start speaking, I honestly don't know how much I'll end up saying. So, if anyone wants to leave midway, they're free to do so."

Kundan didn't respond—meaning Gaurav could continue.

"I want to thank everyone who, despite the pressure of work, still took time to sit with me and just talk. We all work, but informal conversations? That's rare.

I also want to thank this company—because the pressure was so much that it finally made me resign. And a special thanks to whoever came up with *'the idea of a notice period'*. That person, wherever they are, has unknowingly changed my entire life. Because in these last few weeks, I've understood things that most working professionals never do.

It's true that I'm not responsible anymore—because I no longer work to fulfill someone else's wishes. I am not attached to anyone, nor am I the right fit for any job. I have a strong feeling that I'll get fired from my next one too. But I'm happy—because now I've tasted freedom."

Gaurav paused for a second, his tone still calm, almost detached.

"I am on my way to becoming an unpolished stone again. When an uncut stone is chiseled, do you think it feels joy? The joy of turning into a beautiful sculpture? Or the grief of being broken into something else?

So many people believe they are doing it a favor, shaping it into something 'better.' But the truth is—they're not shaping it, they're breaking it.

If you truly want to do it a favor, then just let it be. Let it remain raw, untouched—a mere stone."

His voice was steady, no resentment, just clarity.

"I have no desire to be a robot. I just want to be a proper human. There are already too many robots here—just let me live my life."

There was a brief silence in the room before Gaurav spoke again. This time, his tone softened.

"My daughter is three years old now. But I have only seen her childhood in photographs.

When I leave for work, she's asleep.

When I come back, she's asleep again.

And during this time, I have realized another bitter truth—this system, this pressure, this endless race... it doesn't spare anyone."

The room fell completely silent. Gaurav had been speaking for more than ten minutes now.

No one left the room.

No one disconnected their calls on the teams.

This conversation had become serious—every person in the room was listening intently.

Gaurav picked up the cold drink bottle lying beside him, took a sip, and continued,

"I've seen it. Do you know who ends up taking their own lives the most? Doctors, engineers, IAS, IPS officers—people who have everything, except **peace of mind.**

Every third working professional in India is struggling with **depression** or **anxiety**. The saddest part? Even the ones who smile are often breaking inside.

I was breaking too.

But I owe a big thanks to my friend Kapil. One evening, while having whisky with him, something he said hit me hard.

He looked at me and said, 'I think you've been crushed under so much work pressure that it's affecting your family life.'

That really hit me hard. And just a few days later, when Kundan added more pressure, it gave me the final push—I resigned on the same day. And what came next? My notice period."

Gaurav paused, his voice steady, controlled.

"I've read so many books about **work-life balance**. I tried to build that balance. But the more I tried, the more it started slipping away.

Then I realized—I was walking on a tightrope, suspended in the air. One end tied to the office, the other to my home.

Whenever I tried doing something for myself, the balance would shift. I would slip.

And I would fall.

The bruises from those falls? They were never visible outside—but they hurt the most inside.

Now, that tightrope is gone.

Or maybe, there is no rope at all anymore.

Now, I just have to walk my own way."

Gaurav's voice remained calm, but he added a little emphasis as he spoke next,

"We've always been taught that a job will never let you starve—true. But it's just as true that a job will never let you live either."

The depth of that statement was undeniable. Everyone in the room knew why people worked—to live a comfortable life, to afford good food, good living.

But Gaurav had just pulled the veil off a bitter truth: *A job doesn't let you live either.*

He lowered his voice slightly, keeping it measured.

"Every year, whenever my birthday came...

My wedding anniversary...

Or my daughter's birthday...

There was always some urgent project delivery.

And I would leave those precious moments behind—only to bury myself in Excel sheets and Zoom calls.

9 AM office.

10 AM meeting.

3 PM deadline.

6 PM client call.

And then finally, returning home at 10 PM—completely **drained, exhausted, and guilty.**"

Gaurav let out a small chuckle, a hint of irony in it.

"I know, everyone has 'a boss' breathing down their neck.

That boss has another boss above him.

Then there's the owner.

Then the client.

And then, the 'end-user' breathing down the client's neck.

It's an orbit—that keeps spinning, endlessly."

He took another sip from the bottle before looking straight at Kundan.

"Everyone is tired.

Everyone is stressed.

Everyone says— *'Just a little more money, and 'then' I'll finally live in peace.'*

But that 'then' never comes."

The weight of his words lingered in the room.

Finally, he looked at Kundan and said, his tone still measured, still composed—

"I refused to work on Saturdays and Sundays.

Because of that, I could spend time with my relatives.

I could take out time for myself.

But the employee who replaced me on weekends—his time got wasted, didn't it?

Someone else had to suffer.

If that work had been delivered two days late, would the sky have fallen?

Would the client have had a heart attack?"

Kundan was completely silent. He had nothing to say.

Gaurav continued, his voice calm and measured.

"It doesn't matter. The client only needed to be told that a particular module took longer than expected, and so the delivery would be delayed by two days. I guarantee they would've understood. But no—leaders always find a way to exploit the people below them."

Gaurav turned to General Manager Vipul Bajaj.

"Sir, I've been sharing presentations with you for the last four years. But the one time I didn't, you got upset. You wanted direct credit in front of the client. And let's be honest—whenever a project is delivered, the lead gets all the recognition anyway.

But the moment I tried to take credit for my work? You humiliated me."

Vipul Bajaj said nothing.

Gaurav took a deep breath.

"I don't owe anyone an explanation. I'm not here to preach either. Everyone has their own choices—to work or not work, to stay or quit, to live however they want.

But what I see around me feels strange.

Everyone is saving money for the future.

Yet, everyone is **sacrificing their present** to do it.

It seems like people are losing today, just to worry about tomorrow."

Gaurav glanced at the room full of employees and spoke, "Just a while ago, my leads gave me a scolding. That moment, I realized something.

Quitting is not a weakness. It's courage. It's change.

People will ask me all kinds of questions.

I'll have to stand my ground and answer them."

Gaurav's words hit deep. ***Quitting is not a weakness. It's courage. It's change.***

The meeting was scheduled from 3 to 4 PM. But now, it was already 5.

Gaurav had been speaking for over an hour.

No one had left.

Gaurav took a sip of water and continued.

"The notice period isn't just about informing the company. It's about handing over work.

And in those days, while passing on my projects—I felt empty.

Every day, I handed over one project.

Every day, I felt a little lighter.

When I was handing over work to Shivani, she noticed every single detail.

And that's when I realized something—I too had started **noticing** every single detail in my life.

I noticed...

My daughter is three now.

My silence has made my wife silent too.

I didn't even realize when my parents grew old.

The passions I once had? They now feel like forgotten dreams.

I suddenly saw my old age ahead—just a few years away.

Soon, I'd retire.

And then, regret how life passed by... without ever really living it."

Gaurav took another deep breath.

"But now, I'm noticing my life completely.

A new beginning—where I will truly see my life.

Every day, as if it's the last.

Every relationship, as if it's the first.

These two months—my notice period—were like a pause button on my life.

In these months, I re-learned how to live.

I felt my daughter's laughter.

I saw the same spark in my wife's eyes that was there on our wedding day.

And for the first time, the walls of my house felt warm—not cold and lifeless.

Today is my farewell.

And today, I'm not just leaving my job...

I'm leaving the life I've been living mechanically for years."

Gaurav gave a small smile.

"I think I've taken enough of your time. I should sit now. Thank you all, once again."

Then he turned to Kundan.

"Sir, please arrange for the cold drinks and pizza to be distributed."

Kundan signaled the peon.

As people munched on pizza and sipped their cold drinks, Just then, Kundan asked, "Gaurav, I have one question. Can you please answer it?"

Some people had already started getting up from their chairs.

But the moment Gaurav picked up the mic and said," Yes sure."

Everyone sat back down.

Kundan said, "Gaurav, you spoke about attachment. If I am not attached to my work, how can I perform well?"

Gaurav replied, "You are absolutely right, Kundan Sir. If you are not attached, the work will not be done well. However, this attachment should be by choice—it should come from your genuine desire to be engaged, rather than from compulsion or obligation.

Attachment is important, but it should arise from within, as a conscious decision rather than an imposed necessity. When you willingly connect with your work, it becomes an extension of your aspirations, something that motivates and drives you rather than weighing you down. True attachment should be an act of passion—a force that enhances fulfillment rather than drains your energy.

However, attachment that stems from external pressure—whether societal expectations, financial obligations, or fear of failure—can turn into a burden. Instead of uplifting creativity and productivity, it may lead to frustration, exhaustion, and resentment. When work feels suffocating rather than inspiring, it indicates an attachment born out of necessity rather than choice.

The key is to choose how deeply you engage with your work. If it resonates with your values and fuels your sense of purpose, attachment becomes meaningful—it ceases to be a sacrifice and transforms into an avenue for personal growth. But if you find yourself attached merely out of obligation, it is worth pausing to reassess: ***Is this attachment serving you, or are you serving it?***

So yes, attachment matters, but only the kind that nurtures your enthusiasm rather than diminishes your sense of self."

Kundan asked again, "But what if we don't have a choice, and we're stuck in a job out of necessity? How do we work in such a situation?"

Gaurav explained, "If you're doing a job out of compulsion, the best way is to detach. Detachment doesn't mean being irresponsible; it means setting boundaries. If your job requires nine hours of work, then give it only those nine hours—no more, no less. If you have weekends off, then truly take those days off. Don't carry work stress into your personal time. Use your free time for things that genuinely bring you joy—your hobbies, passions, or simply unwinding with people who matter to you.

If you're working out of necessity, then understand this: at some point, you will leave this job, either because you find something better or because circumstances force you to. So why let it consume your life now? The problem is, when people feel trapped, they start believing that they must surrender completely to their job. They stretch beyond working hours, constantly worry about deadlines, take stress home, and in the process, let their identity get swallowed by their workplace.

I am giving you an example—imagine a waiter working in a restaurant. He's doing the job because he needs the money, not because he's passionate about serving food. But does that mean he should feel miserable all the time? No. He should focus only on his work during his shift and once his duty is over, he should walk out of the restaurant—mentally and physically. He should engage in his own interests, spend time with loved ones, or build something for his future. That way, he's still earning but not letting the job become his entire life.

Detachment is about understanding that your job is just a part of your life, not your whole life. If you detach correctly, you free yourself from unnecessary stress, perform your duties without emotional exhaustion, and keep your personal world intact. And most importantly, you prepare yourself to walk away when the right opportunity comes. "

Kundan was finally beginning to understand. He wasn't angry anymore; instead, he was asking his questions with genuine curiosity. He had tried to grasp Gaurav's perspective before, but something still lingered in his mind—there was one more thing he needed to ask.

He leaned forward slightly in his chair, looking straight at Gaurav. "Let's say I only work for nine hours. But my colleagues work for ten, twelve hours—some even work on their week-offs. If I set boundaries, I'll be the odd one out. Won't they see me as lazy? What if the company fired me for not putting in extra hours? And if I lose my job, how will I manage my expenses, my EMIs, my household needs? What do I do then?"

Gaurav smiled. He glanced at the screen in front of him—many people were listening intently, observing every word being exchanged in the conference room. He shifted his gaze back to Kundan and said, with complete ease, "I knew it. This was the point you were bound to come back to. The real fear—the fear of survival."

He leaned back in his chair, arms relaxed, his tone calm, almost conversational. "Kundan sir, look around you. The answer is right here. If you are working purely out of compulsion, the only way to deal with it is to choose freedom. It's a tough pill to swallow, but it's the only way forward."

He paused for a moment, letting the words settle before continuing. "You think if you don't push yourself beyond your limits, your household will collapse. That without you, everything will stop functioning. But here's the truth—if you die tomorrow, your house will still run. Your family will grieve, they will struggle, but life will go on. Somehow, things will keep moving. That's how life works. So why live like a slave? Why assume that sacrificing your well-being is the only way to sustain yourself?"

The room was silent. His words were hitting hard, but they weren't harsh—they were just brutally honest.

"People stay trapped in this fear forever. They think there's no way out, that they must keep grinding no matter what. But here's what actually happens—one day, after years of compromise, they still lose their job. The company lets them go, their health breaks down, and they realize they never lived for themselves. So why not take control of the situation now?"

He looked straight at Kundan. "You need **courage** to take risks, not blind loyalty to the job. The day you decide you won't let this fear dictate your life, you'll start walking the path of freedom. And trust me, once you start walking that path, you won't turn back."

The tension in the room had changed. People weren't just listening—they were thinking.

Gaurav's words weren't dramatic. They weren't aggressive. They were simply the truth, spoken calmly but powerfully enough to make people question their own realities.

Gaurav continued, his voice steady, his tone calm. "Kundan sir, if you truly want freedom, you need to have the courage for it. If I tell you right now—quit your job and go home—you should have the guts to do it **without hesitation**. The moment you can walk away without fear, that's the moment you truly attain freedom. This isn't just talk. These are deep, unsettling truths. Understanding them............"

His sentence trailed off. Instead of finishing it, he simply stood up. No explanations, no unnecessary words. He didn't acknowledge anyone, didn't try to soften the abruptness—he just walked out of the room.

The conference hall fell silent. People glanced at each other, unsure of what had just happened. No one dared to stop him or ask anything.

Gaurav stepped outside, heading straight to the terrace. The air was cooler now. He pulled out a cigarette, lit it, and took a slow drag, watching the city lights flicker in the distance.

He had changed. There was a time when he would've stayed, would've argued for hours, explaining every nuance, trying to convince people. But now? Now, he was different. Ever since his **Notice Period** had started, something had shifted in him. He had stopped caring about forced conversations, unnecessary debates, or proving a point to people who wouldn't get it anyway.

Before starting the conversation, he had already said,"*I'll speak if I feel like it. If I don't, I'll just stop.*"

It was exactly what had happened.

The cigarette burned down to its last bit. He crushed it under his shoe, exhaled slowly, and checked his watch. 6:00 PM.

Without a second thought, he walked down to the parking area, started his car, and rode off. No messages, no goodbyes.

He had said what he needed to say. The rest, as always, was for people to figure out on their own.

*****

Five days later, Gaurav joined a new company in Manesar, Haryana. It was about an hour and a half from

Patel Nagar, Delhi. He figured a cab would be better than taking his car—less hassle, no parking drama. One trip in a cab would be enough to get a feel for the route and the company vibe.

As expected, the cab ride gave him all the information he needed—the shortcuts, the traffic bottlenecks, the overall ease of commuting. By the end of the day, he knew exactly what to do. From tomorrow, he'll take his own vehicle.

His first interaction was with HR.

"Hi, I'm Gauri," she said, extending her hand.

"Oh, nice to meet you, Gauri," Gaurav replied.

"We've spoken a lot over the phone, but it's good to finally meet in person. Thanks for joining. Let me introduce you to your team lead, Nishant Dube. Come with me."

Gaurav walked alongside her as she led him through the office.

"Mr. Nishant , this is Gaurav. He's joined your team today—it's his first day," Gauri announced.

"Hi, Gaurav. Welcome! Let me introduce you to the rest of the team," Nishant said, shaking his hand.

"Hello, Nishant. Sure," Gaurav responded.

One by one, Nishant introduced him to all fifteen team members. Gaurav listened, nodded, exchanged pleasantries—but his mind was elsewhere. As he sat down at his new desk, he looked around. The office layout, the structure, the hierarchy—everything felt oddly familiar.

"Same setup," he thought. "Team lead, colleagues, HR. A new office, but the same pattern. The same cycle."

Then his eyes landed on Nishant. There was something about him—something uncannily familiar. *"This guy reminds me of Kundan. In fact, he looked like an upgraded version of Kundan. Older. Overworked. Slightly heavier, tired-looking, greying hair, a round belly, thick-rimmed glasses.*

"*Great,*" Gaurav thought, amused. "*Now, instead of Kundan, I have to deal with his father.*"

The entire day had slipped by in a blur of small talks, random greetings, and shallow conversations. One of those days that starts with a plan and ends with you wondering what exactly you did. And just like that, more days passed—each one quietly mocking Gaurav's so-called "terms and conditions" for life.

Nothing had been going according to his rules lately. The work pressure had returned, like an old headache he thought he'd cured. Same endless meetings, same HR nudges, and of course—Nishant, his manager, setting new targets like it was a board game he played every Monday.

It has been close to six months now since Gaurav joined this company. Traffic had become too much, so he started coming to the office by cab every day for the last 6 months.

He sat at his desk, punching in lines of code and wrapping up assignments with the speed and precision people had come to expect from him. That was his reputation—quick, reliable, a finisher. If a task was meant to take twenty days, Gaurav delivered it in fifteen.

But that speed came with a price. Every time he finished early, Nishant handed him more work. Efficiency, in this office, wasn't a virtue—it was a trap.

Just then, his phone buzzed. Yogita.

"Hey, Yogita! Good to hear from you," Gaurav said, a genuine smile lighting up his face for the first time that day.

"I thought you'd never call," she teased. "So I did. How's work treating you?"

"Same old grind. They've started piling on the pressure again. Let's see how long I survive. What about you?"

"I've joined a college," Yogita said, her voice full of something rare—peace. "Went back to Himachal. Remember you told me, create a backup before making a decision? I took that seriously. Tried applying to a bunch of companies—but none gave me the freedom I needed. Then I saw an ad for a computer teacher. Applied. Got selected. Now I teach three classes a day. That's it. Rest of the time—mine."

"That's awesome," Gaurav replied. And he meant every word.

"Did you know Kundan made Sunny the new team lead?" Yogita began, eyes wide with gossip. "And these days he's always hanging out with Shivani. They come to the office together, leave together, and even have lunch side by side." She went on, spilling everything like old memories rushing back.

Gaurav gave a half-smile. "Well, of course Kundan had to make Sunny the lead. After all, Sunny's got direct links with the senior manager. The manager practically treats him like a son. He'll retire from this company with a nameplate on his desk and a plant on the side. Not like he's got the spine to make it outside on his own."

Yogita giggled, then shifted the topic. "By the way, what's Kapil up to these days? Haven't seen him around much. Ever since his wedding last month, he barely speaks to anyone."

Gaurav chuckled. "Typical post-marriage syndrome. Happens to the best of us. Even at home, freedom gets... reassigned."

The word "freedom" landed differently. Gaurav suddenly fell silent. For a moment, it was like someone had hit pause in his brain. He realized he was slipping back into that locked-in zone—the one he had escaped during his notice period, the one he swore he wouldn't return to. But somewhere in the rush of deadlines, he had allowed the pressure to creep in again.

"What happened?" Yogita asked, her voice gentle. "You went quiet."

"Nothing," he said, but his eyes betrayed a drift—as if a part of him had wandered off to someplace calmer.

They spoke for a while after that. Shared a few jokes. Laughed at some old office gossip. And for the first time in days, Gaurav felt a little lighter. Like maybe the world wasn't always out to get him.

But that fragile peace shattered in seconds.

They were still on the call when Nishant waved from across the floor, not even pretending to care about the ongoing conversation.

Nishant, standing across the floor, signaled at him sharply—'Come now.'

Gaurav held up his hand—'Five minutes.'

That was enough to poke the bear. Nishant marched over to his desk, voice raised for everyone to hear.

"When a manager calls, you don't sit on phone calls like a college kid. I've been watching you for the last fifteen minutes. I've got urgent changes to get done—this doesn't bother you at all, does it?"

Gaurav slowly placed the phone down. And then—like thunder in his brain—came a flash of something he'd told Kundan, not too long ago.

"If you really want freedom, stand up and leave. Right now. No drama. Just go."

And now here he was—sitting there like a hypocrite. Giving others courage while secretly clutching his own fears.

Did I ever walk the path I told Kundan to take? Or have I just been pretending all along? Am I really free—or just stuck with nicer chains?

He stood up.

Looked Nishant dead in the eye and said, "Congratulations on your job. You can keep it."

Then, right there—still standing—he opened his laptop. Typed two words into his resignation email:

Subject: Resignation

Body: Bye-bye.

He didn't say a word. No explanations, no goodbyes. He simply walked out.

Just like that.

Sometimes, freedom isn't about a big declaration. It's just... one step. Out the door.

Outside, **he waited for the cab,** the breeze brushing against his face as he gazed into the open sky. A quiet calm settled over him—weightless, like a moment caught between endings and beginnings.

He was thinking to do all this: *"I will go to the cricket ground. A group of young boys would already be there, gathered for their regular coaching session. He'd pick up a ball, smile, and join them.*

I've got a financial backup that can last me five years now. So even if I earn less by giving cricket coaching, I can still do it happily.

That was it. No corporate meetings. No forced formalities. Just cricket. Just freedom.

And for the first time in a long time, his mind was exactly where he wanted it to be."

THE GUILT
By: Mohan Bachhety

Enter Caption

SHADOW CHASING SHADOW
MOHAN BACHHETY

Enter Caption

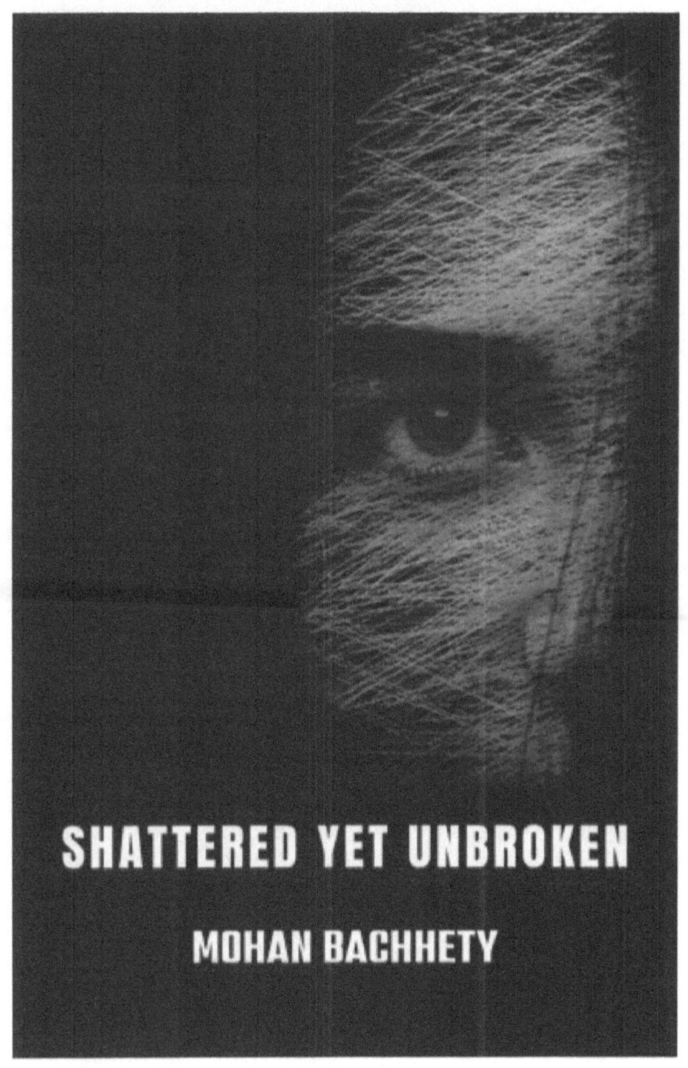

SHATTERED YET UNBROKEN
MOHAN BACHHETY

Enter Caption

Enter Caption

The Day
Happiness
Found Me !
- Mausoleum of Happiness
Mohan Bachhety

Enter Caption

Enter Caption